## "What's going on under there?" a masculine voice demanded

Summers straightened instinctively, striking her head. "Aaiii!" she yelped. Derek Anderson had no right to be in her bedroom, much less to catch her crawling on her belly under her bed!

Sputtering indignantly and rubbing her scalp, Summer emerged to find Derek smiling at her. "I just came by to ask if you've been getting all the gifts I sent," he murmured soothingly.

Glaring at him, she nodded, then asked suspiciously, "So what was the empty envelope for?"

"Ah, yes, that's the other reason I'm here. I had to deliver the contents in person so I wouldn't be jealous of the messenger...."

And as Summer stiffened again in indignation, he leaned over and kissed her...thoroughly.

**Gina Wilkins**'s idea for *Hero in Disguise* came to her in Rose Bud, Arkansas, during a camping trip that was supposed to be a holiday from writing. Overcome by inspiration, Gina scribbled madly at picnic tables, in fishing boats and on the beach while her husband and their two daughters carried on around her. Before the four-day trip ended, Gina had completed the story line. "The only part of the camping trip I remember," she says, "was trying to write by the glow of plastic lanterns." We in Temptation urge this talented new writer to "keep on camping!"

Gina lives in Jacksonville, Arkansas.

# *Hero in Disguise*

## GINA WILKINS

# *Harlequin Books*

TORONTO • NEW YORK • LONDON
AMSTERDAM • PARIS • SYDNEY • HAMBURG
STOCKHOLM • ATHENS • TOKYO • MILAN

For John, whose love gave me courage,
and for Terry, a very special friend.

Published October 1987

ISBN 0-373-25274-9

# 1

"OH, MY GOD, what is *he* doing here?"

Connie's distressed query drew Summer's attention away from the noisy, uninhibited party going on in their living room. She turned her eyes toward the open doorway. Her pulse gave an odd little leap at the sight of the attractive man standing there looking curiously around the crowded room. Surrounded by movement and color, he was conspicuous by his very stillness and neutrality. He looked to be in his late thirties and was dressed quite conservatively in a tan sport coat and dark brown slacks, a muted striped tie knotted at the collar of his cream shirt.

"Bill collector?" she inquired of her obviously displeased roommate.

"Worse," Connie groaned. "It's Derek."

"*That's* your brother?" Summer asked in surprise, her eyebrows shooting upward to disappear beneath her heavy fringe of amber-brown bangs. "What's he doing here?"

"That's what I want to know. He's lived across the bay from us for six months and he has to pick tonight, of all nights, to pay a surprise visit," Connie muttered grimly. "And I was having such a good time," she added in a wail. Squaring her shoulders beneath her brilliantly patterned, oversize sweatshirt, she tossed her unruly red hair out of her face and started across the room toward her older brother.

Summer found herself unable to look away from Derek Anderson. Because Connie and Derek had been at odds since he had settled in Sausalito six months earlier, Summer had not had the chance to meet Connie's brother before that night. He looked nothing like the mental picture she had formed of him. Connie had always described her older brother as average in appearance, stern of personality. Summer had expected to meet a man who looked older than his thirty-seven years, dull and unappealing. That was not what she saw as she stared at him. True, Derek's tobacco-brown hair was conservatively short, his black-framed glasses quite conventional and his clothing rather staid. But there was something about him that didn't conform to Summer's preconceptions. Something about the spark of streetwise intelligence in pewter-gray eyes when they met hers for a moment from across the room. Or the six feet of hard, lean muscle beneath the strictly tailored clothing where there should have been softness and perhaps a little flab. Or maybe it was something about those broad, squared shoulders.

He looked strong, solid, a little tough. Even as she watched him conversing stiffly with his defensive sister, Summer decided that there was more to this man than Connie had implied. Never one to resist a challenge, Summer vowed to make an effort to find out more about Derek Anderson—personally—at the earliest opportunity.

"Hey, Summer," someone said, drawing her attention reluctantly away from her roommate's possibly interesting brother. "Tell Clay about the ninety-year-old dude who tried to pick you up in the supermarket the other day."

"Ninety?" she scoffed, her brilliant blue eyes widening dramatically. "He was a hundred if he was a day." Then, with great enthusiasm and liberal embellishment, she launched into a mostly apocryphal account that soon had her listeners bellowing with laughter. Her own laughter, which had once been described by an infatuated and quickly dispatched young man as "the tinkling of dozens of fairy bells," floated frequently above the less refined guffaws.

"What are you doing here, Derek?" Connie demanded the moment she came to a stop in front of him.

"I wanted to meet some of your friends," her brother replied in a conciliatory voice. "I heard you mention this party to Mom last weekend and I thought this would be a good opportunity for us to interact socially."

"Did it ever occur to you to request an invitation?" Connie asked him sarcastically, her green eyes glittering. "And don't give me that stuff about interacting socially. You're just here to criticize my friends and make more cutting remarks about the way I run my life."

Derek sighed. "Would you give me a break, Connie? I'm trying to offer a truce."

"Sure you are. The same way you 'offer' advice, right?"

Derek ran his fingers through his short brown hair in frustration. "You want me to leave?"

"Suit yourself," Connie answered with a shrug. "I'm sure you'll be bored to tears. Don't expect me to entertain you. I plan to spend the evening with my friends." She placed extra emphasis on the last word.

Derek was tempted to tell his sister that she was acting like a brat but knew that comment would not help matters between them. "I'll stay for a while, then," he told her. "And I won't expect you to entertain me."

Connie shrugged again. "Whatever."

He refused to allow her to make him angry. Instead, he looked around the crowded room, pausing when his gaze clashed with a pair of vivid blue eyes. "Who's the woman on the bar stool?" he asked, hardly aware of having spoken aloud.

"That's my roommate," Connie answered coolly. "Summer Reed. You've heard me talk about her. Go introduce yourself if you want to. I'm going to mingle with my guests." She didn't add "invited guests," but then she really didn't have to. Her tone said it for her.

Not for the first time, Derek was aware of a sense of regret that his absence from the country for most of the past fifteen years had left such a rift between him and his only sibling. A rift that he was having no luck trying to repair. He'd had some vague notion of getting closer to his estranged sister by meeting some of her friends and learning more about her life-style, of which he frankly disapproved. Unfortunately, he'd made her angry again. He seemed to have a real talent for it, he thought, stifling a sigh. Connie was convinced that he was there only to criticize her.

Looking around, Derek was relieved to discover that the admittedly eccentric group of young people with whom Connie claimed friendship was not quite as un-savory as he had expected. True, alcohol was flowing freely, but no one seemed to be indulging more than the usual overly enthusiastic party guest, and Derek saw no sign of illegal substances being used. The music was too loud, the clothing decidedly strange and the hu-mor rather twisted, but on the whole he saw nothing more detrimental than the quite obvious signs of immaturity and irresponsibility.

Derek's attention wandered back toward the battered wooden bar across the room. Specifically he focused on the young woman chatting animatedly from the only bar stool. His immediate attraction to Summer had startled him. She was too young for him, for one thing. He knew she was Connie's age—twenty-five, twelve years younger than Derek. She wasn't particularly glamorous. Her short, silky hair was golden brown, her eyes bright blue, her face lovely in a refreshingly wholesome way. She seemed to wear a permanent smile, a wide, contagious grin that displayed very even white teeth and a glimpse of pink tongue. Because he was consumed by a sudden hunger to have that smile turned upon him, Derek straightened his tie and moved deliberately toward the bar.

The floor of the large living area of the furnished apartment had been cleared for dancing—no big deal since the only furniture consisted of a sagging couch and a couple of small, worn armchairs flanked by a rickety coffee table and two mismatched end tables. Music throbbed from the stereo system in one corner. Still perched on the stool beside the functional bar, Summer sipped her liberally spiked punch, watching what promised to become a hilarious dance contest. Clay McEntire—Crazy Clay—was in rare form that night, and Summer was fully prepared to enjoy the show.

"Has the queen bee been deserted by her drones?" a dry voice inquired from her side. Though not raised above the screaming music, the words were clearly audible nonetheless.

Summer looked around with an eyebrow lifted in curiosity to find Derek Anderson leaning negligently against the bar beside her. "I beg your pardon?"

"You've been sitting here surrounded by an audience since I arrived. What are you to keep them so entertained, a stand-up comic?"

"A sit-down comic, actually," Summer replied in her soft Southern drawl, resisting the impulse to rub her right knee. "How are you, Derek? I'm Connie's roommate, Summer Reed."

"Yes, I know. I hope you don't mind that I crashed your party tonight."

"Of course not. I'm glad you're here. I've wanted to meet my all-time favorite roomie's brother. Connie's told me a lot about you."

"I'm sure she has." His voice was heavy with irony, his pewter eyes entirely too knowing. "Has she told you that 'Derek the Dictator' is a sanctimonious, interfering stuffed shirt?"

Summer grinned. "That about sums it up."

Derek's eyes slid slowly down to her smile, and Summer was rather surprised to feel a momentary self-consciousness at the intensity of his close regard. Though Derek's expression seemed admiring enough, she was under no illusion that he was bowled over by her beauty. She wasn't beautiful. Her hair, the color of clear amber honey, was cut very short in the back and left longer in the front to fall in a flirty fringe over her intensely blue eyes. The rest of her features, in Summer's opinion, were rather ordinarily pixieish—a small, tip-tilted nose, high cheekbones and a generous smile. No dimples, thank God. She'd always thought that dimples would have made her just too "cute" to bear.

She crossed her denim-covered legs and returned Derek's unblinking look. "I've always wondered how accurate Connie's description of you was," she informed him with a suggestion of a question mark at the end of the comment. She especially wondered now, as she found herself responding to his hard strength in a decidedly physical way, if all those derogatory remarks Connie had made in the past few months had been anywhere near the truth. Summer had certainly never expected to find herself attracted to the man, yet her quickened breathing and accelerated heartbeat as he leaned closer made it impossible for her to deny that she was. "Are you really as bossy as she says?"

His breath almost brushing the soft cheek of the woman on the tall stool beside him, Derek seemed to reflect a moment, then his hard mouth twisted into a smile of sorts. "I suppose she was fairly accurate."

There was just something about him.... Summer eyed him consideringly. "I wonder."

Seeming to suddenly grow tired of the subject of himself, Derek nodded toward the writhing bodies on the makeshift dance floor. "I know why I'm not out there making an idiot of myself, but what about you? Why aren't you dancing?"

Summer shrugged, unable this time to keep herself from protectively cupping her knee. "I'm just not into dancing. Tell me about the new business you've started, Derek. Management consulting, isn't it?"

"Yes, that's right. I'm specializing in small, struggling businesses."

Though he didn't elaborate, Summer knew that Derek was already making a name for himself in his field. In spite of herself, Connie had not quite been able to hide her pride in her brother's early success. He was not yet rich from his new enterprise, nor was he known in any part of the country other than Marin County and the surrounding San Francisco area, but Connie seemed to think it was only a matter of time. Examining the determined glint in Derek's gray eyes, Summer knew Connie was probably right. This was a man who could accomplish whatever he desired.

She peeked at Derek through her lashes as she lifted her punch and took a sip. "You must be very good at what you do."

He looked at her suspiciously. "Why?"

She returned the look innocently. "Connie tells me that you're an expert on offering advice." Connie had been quite vocal in her displeasure with Derek's heavily paternal treatment of her. She'd informed Summer that Derek offered advice to struggling businessmen during working hours and to his resentful younger sister in the little free time his career left him.

Derek winced, obviously well aware of his sister's opinion of his "advice." "I think I'll pour myself a drink."

Summer laughed softly. "Why don't you do that? Would you like some punch? It's pretty good, though God only knows what's in it."

"No, thanks. I'll pass." He reached for a bottle of Scotch, splashing a generous amount over two ice cubes in a glass that looked suspiciously like a jelly jar.

Summer exhaled dramatically. "Okay, we'll drop the subject of your present career. How about your former one? Were you truly just a government gofer, as Connie likes to say, or were you really something more exciting, like a spy?" Actually, Connie had been rather vague about what Derek had done for the fifteen years prior to settling in Sausalito, but Summer had understood that he'd worked in some sort of diplomatic capacity that had kept him on the move from one American embassy to another.

Derek answered without changing expression. "A spy, of course. But I try not to spread that around."

Delighted with his answer, since it indicated that he did possess a sense of humor, Summer smiled brightly. "Of course not. Tell me, Derek, was it terribly exciting?"

"Terribly."

"And chillingly dangerous?"

"Chillingly."

"And desperately romantic?"

"Desperately."

She laughed and leaned against the bar, cocking her head to meet his studiously grave expression with a friendly smile. "You have such a colorful way with words, Derek. Are all spies as silver-tongued as you?"

He nodded. "Just like James Bond."

"Why in the world would you leave such an exciting life to become an ordinary California businessman?" she asked tauntingly.

He shoved one hand into the pocket of his brown slacks and leaned beside her, his drink held loosely in his other hand. He continued to watch her with that oddly intense gaze as he answered lightly, "All that excitement, danger and romance gets boring after a while. I needed a change."

"How fascinating." So he was capable of returning nonsense for nonsense, Summer thought in fascination. Connie hadn't mentioned that. In fact, Summer added reflectively, her eyes straying to Derek's powerful chest and muscular thighs, there were several things about her brother that Connie had failed to mention. She decided it was time to test his reflexes. "So, Derek, Connie tells me now that you've retired from globe-trotting, you've decided to settle down and become domesticated. Looking for a wife?"

He had just taken a sip of his Scotch. For a moment Summer thought he might choke, and she watched expectantly. Instead, he swallowed, set his glass on the bar and leaned even closer so that his chest brushed her shoulder. "Perhaps," he agreed. "Are you applying for the position?"

Summer chuckled and lifted her plastic tumbler in a mock salute. "Good comeback, Derek."

She imagined that his almost imperceptible smile was reflected in his metallic eyes. "Maybe I was serious."

"I think you should know I'm not exactly good wife material."

"Why not?" he inquired, looking admirably unfazed by the personal nature of his conversation with this impish stranger.

She lifted her watermelon-painted fingertips and began to enumerate. "A respectable businessman-type such as you would want someone punctual, fond of schedules. I'm neither. I'm not particularly well educated. I dropped out of college in the second semester of my sophomore year. The only thing I'm serious about is not being serious. I'm not socially or professionally ambitious. I require a great deal of attention and I like being entertained. Connie says you're a real sports nut. The only sports I participate in are people-watching and an occasional card game—for fun, of course. Do I sound like the woman you've been looking for?"

"No," he answered genially. "You don't sound at all like the woman I've been looking for. Perhaps I've been looking for the wrong kind of woman."

Summer's smile grew even more brilliant, though she wished rather breathlessly that he would step back just a little. She was entirely too aware of the feel of him against her shoulder. "I like you, Derek Anderson," she told him candidly. "Connie forgot to mention that her brother can be charming when he chooses to be. You and I might even manage to become friends."

The suggestion of a smile faded abruptly from Derek's eyes. "I can't seem to accomplish that feat even with my own sister."

Summer caught the undercurrents of pain in his voice. "I don't think Connie knows that you *want* to be her friend," she told him carefully.

He exhaled through his straight, sharply carved nose and changed the subject. "So what kind of man are you looking for, since you've turned up your nose at respectable businessmen? Or are you looking?"

Swallowing another sip of her punch, Summer swung one leg in time to the music pounding over their conversation and replied, "Not actively. I'm waiting for the kind of hero Bonnie Tyler describes in her song, and they seem to be in short supply."

A slight frown creased Derek's brow behind his dark-framed glasses. "What song?"

"Sorry. I should have known you aren't into rock and roll. It's called 'Holding Out For a Hero.'"

"Oh. So what special qualities must this 'hero' possess?"

A flippant grin punctuating her words, she responded lightly. "Well, for starters, he has to have a great sense of humor. And he has to be adventurous and occasionally impulsive yet always there when I need him. I'd want him to be kind and caring, strong in more than the physical sense and emotionally mature. Like I said, there aren't many of them around."

Derek studied her face. "I thought you only wanted to party. Doesn't seem like you should want anyone to be beside you in times of trouble if you don't *have* times of trouble," he pointed out.

"Everyone has times of trouble. Times when it would be nice to have someone to lean on," Summer answered, unaware that her eyes had filled with an old, distant sadness as she thought back five years to a time when she had needed someone and to a man who had not been there for her. Then, realizing that she was allowing the conversation to become too heavy, she pasted her best party-girl smile back on her animated face and added, "Even Minnie Mouse has good old Mickey."

Derek's eyes gleamed with a sudden inner smile. "You're saying your hero is Mickey Mouse?"

She laughed. "Close enough." With the conversation back on a light line she was much more comfortable, able to throw off the past.

"Maybe the problem is that you've been dating the wrong kind of men. Maybe you should try dating men who are more—"

"Like you? Thanks, but no thanks," she quipped, though she wondered what she would say if he did ask her out. She wasn't sure she'd be able to turn him down, particularly if he was standing as close to her as he was now.

"Have I just been insulted? What's wrong with men like me? I'm emotionally mature, and I'm particularly good in times of trouble."

"I'm sure you are, but you're entirely too proper and conventional. I know it drives you crazy that Connie quit school and has no career goals and that she never misses a chance to party. You just can't resist offering her advice on how to improve her life. Like Connie, I would frustrate someone like you, and I would get tired of always being expected to follow your suggestions. A real hero for me would be a cross between you and...and someone like Clay McEntire over there." She pointed to a rugged, blond jock-type who was doing a really funny impersonation of a Motown backup singer as an oldie from The Temptations played in the background.

Following the direction of her pointing finger, Derek grunted and shook his head. "I'd jump feetfirst into a tar pit before I'd make a spectacle of myself like he's doing," he admitted. "Wouldn't it bother you to put on that kind of performance?"

"Oh, I've given a few performances in my time. Sometime Clay and I will have to show you our special impression of Gladys Knight and One Pip," she answered humorously. "You can't have any fun if you're stiff and formal all the time, Derek."

"Fun," he replied thoughtfully. "You call this party fun?"

"Very much so," she answered decisively. "Do you really dislike it all that much?"

"No." He looked directly into her eyes. "Not at all."

She started to ask him to elaborate, then decided not to. His proximity was doing unusual things to her senses, and suddenly words eluded her—an odd experience for Summer Reed, who always had a ready quip on her lips. She could smell the crisp after-shave Derek wore and see the sheen of tanned flesh where the

indirect lighting of the room fell on his face and throat.
She was also becoming inexplicably fascinated by his
eyes, their color changing from dull pewter when he
was serious to a gleaming silver when they reflected the
smile that barely touched his stern mouth. She was becoming more and more aware of his physical attri-
butes, which she found rather dismaying.

"Are you actually admitting that it's okay to enjoy a
party?" she asked him quickly, forcing her voice
through her tight throat.

"Occasionally," he replied. "But there's no excuse for
making it one's only purpose for living as my sister
seems to do."

Summer straightened defensively on her stool, glaring at the man beside her without a trace of her lovely
smile. "Connie is my best friend, Derek Anderson, and
she's a terrific person. Sure she's made a few mistakes
in her life, but who hasn't? You should consider yourself lucky to have her for a sister rather than trying to
change her into your idea of the perfect young woman."

"That's telling him, Summer." Standing just behind
Summer's shoulder, Connie applauded her roommate's indignant speech. Her improbably red hair worn
in a shaggy semipunk style and her green eyes outlined
liberally with kohl, Connie looked even younger than
her twenty-five years in her baggy sweatshirt, which
hung almost to the knees of her skintight black leg-
gings. She could not have made a more startling contrast to her brother's conservative attire. "I should have
warned you, Derek, my friend Summer won't be any
more hesitant about telling you off than I am. You don't
intimidate everyone, you know."

"I never tried to intimidate you, Connie."

Watching in silence, Summer thought she detected a shade of sadness in Derek's eyes. She believed that he truly wanted what was best for his sister, though he couldn't seem to accept that Connie had a right to her own mistakes. She turned her eyes to Connie and recognized the wistfulness in her friend's voice when she answered. "You just refuse to believe that I'm completely happy the way I am, don't you, Derek? You won't let me forget the mess I made of my marriage to Stu, as if none of it would have happened if I had only listened to you.

"But how could I have listened to you, Derek? Where were you when I was seventeen and madly infatuated with a handsome young actor? Somewhere in Europe or Southeast Asia or the Middle East, giving advice, as usual. I never saw you, I hardly ever heard from you and yet I was supposed to conform exactly to your expectations for me. Well, forget it, Derek. I'll do just fine without your advice now, just as I always have before. And if you're disappointed with what I've become in the fifteen years since you went off in search of adventure, that's just tough."

"Connie—"

"Hey, Connie!" someone yelled from across the room. "Come on, let's dance."

"I'm on my way," Connie yelled back, then tilted her head defiantly, looking at Derek even as she called across the room, "Let's party till we drop! Who wants more punch?"

"All right! Bring on the punch!"

Spinning on one heel, Connie threw herself back into the party with what Summer sensed was a desperate act of defiance. Summer ached for her friend, whose self-confidence and self-image had been so badly damaged by her failed teenage marriage. Connie would never admit those weaknesses, just as Summer found it hard to reveal her own insecurities and vulnerabilities to others, but the buried scars were there, in both of the determinedly cheerful young women.

Summer also felt rather sorry for Derek, whose face had gone hard but whose eyes were still so sad. "Can't you just accept her the way she is, Derek?" she asked suddenly, wanting to help despite her reluctance to get involved in a family matter. "You said you wanted to be her friend. Give her a chance to show you what a wonderful person she is."

"Now who's offering advice?" he questioned her shortly, then sighed. "Sorry. Listen, I think I'll cut out now. I've had about all of this 'fun' I can take."

For some strange reason Summer was reluctant to see him leave, but no hint of that reluctance was allowed to creep into her voice as she responded. "All right. I'm glad we had the opportunity to meet tonight, Derek. Perhaps we'll see each other again soon."

Derek turned his attention away from his sister to give Summer another one of those intense, unsettling looks. "You can count on it," he told her. Then he drained the last of his Scotch and started across the room toward the door. Before he reached it, Bonnie Tyler's wonderfully sandpapery voice sounded from the speakers in the chorus of "Holding Out For a Hero." Summer had been watching his departure, so she was looking straight into his eyes when he turned, jerked his head toward the stereo to indicate that he'd recognized the words, then lifted two fingers in a kind of salute before he disappeared through the door.

Nice, Summer thought. Strong. Dependable. Too bad he was so darned proper.

"Well, what did you think of my brother?" Connie asked later. "You two certainly talked for a long time. Wasn't he just the way I described?"

"Oh, I don't know," Summer answered vaguely. "I think you might be underestimating him, Connie. He's not as stern and inflexible as you've told me he is."

"Uh-oh. Don't tell me *you've* been taken in by his embassy charm."

"I like him, Connie—for a respectable businessman-type. I think he's unhappy about the distance between you. He implied that he'd like to be your friend."

Connie snorted bitterly. "Friends accept each other the way they are, like you and I do, Summer. They don't try to change each other."

"Maybe Derek will figure that out for himself before long. Give him a chance," Summer urged, repeating the words she'd used to Derek. "After all, he's only been back in the country for a few months after being away for most of your life. You've hardly seen him during those years, so the two of you have had to start almost as strangers."

"He still treats me as if I were ten years old," Connie complained. "I'm so tired of him telling me that I could do better for myself than what I'm doing."

"Give it time, Connie. He's trying."

"I'll try," Connie sighed. "It would please my parents if Derek and I learned to get along better," she added, as if it really didn't matter to her one way or the other. Then she rushed back into the middle of the party, obviously intending to put her brother completely out of her mind.

Summer shook her head in sympathy, never asking how two siblings could be so different. After all, her own family was a good example of the same phenomenon. Summer's two lovely sisters were as different from each other as they were from Summer.

But Summer and Connie—now *they* were a well-matched pair. Summer had liked Connie Anderson from the day she'd first met her in the accounting office where they both worked. They loved to laugh together, and their sense of humor was almost identical. They enjoyed music, parties, people and comedy clubs. They both hid any fears or doubts they might carry inside them behind quick wits and ready smiles, each having her own good reasons for doing so.

Their only major difference was their approach to men. Trying to bolster her bruised ego, Connie flitted from one man to another with all the discrimination of a starving honeybee in a field of wildflowers. Summer dated frequently and enjoyed the company of men, but few of the relationships she'd tentatively entered during the past five years had progressed beyond friendship. She maintained that she was waiting for a flawless fairy-tale hero—though she knew she would never find one—which was her method of protecting herself from the type of pain and disillusionment she had experienced five years earlier. Only to herself would she admit she wouldn't really know what to do with a fairy-tale hero if she found one. She suspected that a truly perfect man would make her all too aware of her own imperfections, as well as boring her to tears.

Other than that one relatively unimportant diversity, Summer and Connie could have hatched from the same egg. They continued to work in their uninspiring, undemanding jobs only to finance their more pleasurable pastimes, were the despair of their families and employers and the delight of their many friends.

All in all, Summer reflected contentedly, fate had been very kind to allow her path to cross Connie Anderson's.

She had no idea of how fate had capriciously decided to bring Connie's brother into Summer's life, as well.

# 2

SUMMER CAME partially awake with a muffled groan, reached out a hand and slapped at her alarm clock. When that failed to stop the persistent chiming that had disturbed her, she groped for the telephone receiver and pulled it to her ear. "Hello? What is it?" she demanded hoarsely, then glared at the instrument when it responded to her impatient question with a monotonous dial tone. Finally waking enough to realize that the chimes were the result of a determined finger pressed to the doorbell, she muttered an unladylike curse and snatched up her lightweight robe.

"Who on earth would be ringing my doorbell at eight o'clock on a Saturday morning?" she grumbled, stumbling across the party-littered living room to the door. "Derek!" she exclaimed in surprise, throwing open the door to reveal the impatient-looking man in the hallway. "What are you doing here?" And how could anyone look so crisp and alert at this hour of the morning? she added silently.

His gray eyes leisurely surveying her tumbled hair, sleep-blurred features and bedroom attire, Derek answered, "I'm here to see Connie. Is she still sleeping?"

"I'm sure she is," Summer replied, leaning weakly against the edge of the door she held open. The slow, thorough journey of his eyes from the top of her head to her bare toes had affected her as if it had been his hand that had examined her, leaving her feeling a little shaken. God, it was too early in the morning to deal with this type of sensation. She hadn't even had her coffee yet!

"Would you mind waking her?" Derek asked quietly in that gravelly voice that was like a sandpaper caress to her senses. "I thought I would take her out for breakfast."

Summer's habit had always been to lighten a tense moment with a wisecrack. Since Derek was making her decidedly uncomfortable with his unblinking pewter regard of her, she grinned impishly. "My goodness, is this an impulsive action?" she asked in mock astonishment, then continued without allowing him to respond. "It's very nice of you, but you'd need an airplane to get to her before lunch. Connie's in Los Angeles."

Derek looked startled, and Summer imagined that one did not often catch that particular expression on his stern face. "Los Angeles? How can that be? I left her here less than ten hours ago."

"You left the party only a couple of hours before Connie left for L.A."

Derek ran an impatient hand through his tobacco-brown hair and attempted to make sense of the conversation. "My sister left for Los Angeles at midnight?" he asked slowly.

"That's right. Please come in, Derek, and I'll make us some coffee. I find it very hard to give explanations before I've had my caffeine fix."

"I gathered there was some reason for our lack of communication," Derek commented dryly. He took a step forward. Since Summer had not yet moved aside to allow him entrance into the apartment, she found herself suddenly standing so close to his sturdy chest that she could almost feel the rise and fall of his breath.

Instinct told her to move hastily backward, but her reflexes seemed to be unusually slow. She stayed right where she was, staring into Derek's unrevealing gray eyes like a paralyzed rabbit into bright headlights. Did she imagine it, or did something suddenly flicker in those silvery depths? Something dangerous and infinitely exciting.

"You are rather slow before you've had your coffee, aren't you?" Derek murmured, and Summer imagined that his voice was a little rougher than usual. She took an awkward step backward, giving him just enough room to enter the apartment, his arm brushing her as he passed. Suppressing a quiver at the momentary contact, Summer closed the door and leaned against it, watching as Derek looked around the cluttered room with a slight moue of distaste. "Connie left you with the mess, I see," he commented.

Summer cleared her throat soundlessly. "I told her I didn't mind. I had nothing better to do this morning." Her eyes wandered from his face, idly approving the lean strength beneath his crisp white shirt and sharply creased navy slacks. "Do you always dress so conservatively for a Saturday morning, or is this the proper attire for escorting one's sister to breakfast?" she asked with deceptively mild curiosity, retreating again behind a facetious remark. "Do you even own a sweatshirt or a pair of jeans?"

"You're hardly in a position to criticize *my* appearance," Derek returned, eyeing her with an enigmatic half smile. Her short golden-brown hair was wildly disarrayed, and one recalcitrant lock stood straight up at her crown. She'd made a halfhearted effort to remove her makeup before falling into bed at three o'clock that morning, but there were still faint smudges of mascara on the fair, smooth skin beneath her heavy-lidded eyes. The garishly flowered pink-and-green satin kimono she wore clashed appallingly with the silky legs of her pumpkin-colored pajamas. She was hardly dressed for seduction. Yet his entire body was taut, vibrating with a sudden surge of desire for her. He shoved his fists into his pockets to loosen the front of his snugly tailored slacks, his dark brows drawing downward in self-annoyance.

"I'll change after I've had my coffee," Summer answered with a shrug, unaware of Derek's problem. "Can you tolerate instant, or should I brew a pot?"

"I'll make the coffee. You go wash your face. You look like a panda bear. Cute but distracting." Definitely distracting. Those soft smudges made his fingers itch to smooth them away. He needed a few minutes alone to remind himself of all the logical reasons that he should not take advantage of his sister's absence to make a move on her attractive roommate.

When Summer didn't immediately respond to his suggestion, Derek reached out with a faint smile to give her a light push in the direction of her bedroom. Since she had been precariously balanced on one foot, the other crossed in front of her, his slight shove caused her to wobble. Before Derek could make a grab to steady her, she fell to one knee, gasping in pain as she made contact with the uncarpeted wood floor.

"Summer, I'm sorry." Derek was sincerely contrite as he knelt beside her to help her to her feet. "I certainly never meant to—"

"I know you didn't," she interrupted him, brushing off his apology. Clutching his arm, she rose slowly, flexing the offending knee when she was upright. "Don't worry about it, Derek. It was simply an accident. I told you I'm not at my best before my coffee."

"Are you all right? You look a little pale." He had an arm around her shoulders for support.

Much more aware of his nearness than the ache in her knee, Summer swallowed and shrugged casually out of his supportive embrace. "I'm fine. I just landed on an old war injury," she told him lightly. "Go make the coffee, Derek, while I remove my 'cute but distracting' panda mask."

Partially reassured by her airy dismissal, Derek nodded and stepped away from her, though his eyes frowned steadily at her back as she moved toward her bedroom. She had taken only three steps when his exclamation of distress stopped her. "Dammit, Summer, you're limping! I really hurt you, didn't I?" Before she could open her mouth to deny his self-recrimination, he had swept her into his arms as if she weighed nothing and was carrying her to the worn sofa, which was still shoved against one wall.

"Derek, will you put me down!" Summer gasped, clutching at his shoulder for balance. Lord, he was strong. And so warm. His warmth scorched her through her thin nightclothes. "You did *not* hurt me. I *always* limp," she told him as evenly as she could under the circumstances.

She was completely ignored as Derek deposited her with great care in the center of the sagging couch and, holding her leg still with a hand at her ankle, began to roll up her wide pajama leg. "Derek! Stop that!" She reached down to arrest his hand, reluctant for him to see her leg, but he easily overpowered her.

"Dear God, Summer, what did you do to this knee?" Derek stared in near horror at the slender appendage, which was disfigured by a veritable spiderweb of scars from her lower thigh to two inches below her knee. The kneecap itself was unnaturally lopsided.

"If you had listened to me instead of throwing me around like a sack of potatoes, I would have told you," she answered crossly, not caring that her analogy bore little resemblance to his somewhat high-handed but unarguably gentle handling of her. She looked away from the expression on his face, not wanting to see the revulsion that usually followed the shock.

"I'm listening now."

"I was injured in a motorcycle accident five years ago. A car ran a stop sign and smashed into me. I'll walk with this limp for the rest of my life, but since I nearly had to have the leg amputated, I'm not complaining. Now are you satisfied that you did not cause me a terrible injury?"

Still holding her leg just behind the knee, Derek sat back on his heels and looked intently up at her. "How'd the guy driving the motorcycle fare?"

"*I* was driving the motorcycle, you chauvinist. And the accident wasn't my fault." She wished she could control the slight trembling of her muscles beneath his warm palm. With uncharacteristic bitterness she told herself he must not be aware that he was still holding the disfigured leg. It was hardly a sight to make him want to touch her.

"How long did it take you to get back on your feet?"

"Almost two years," Summer admitted reluctantly, desperately wishing he'd move his hand. "I spent some time in bed, then in a wheelchair, then using a walker and crutches. I skipped having to use a cane, though."

"Good for you. I have a feeling you hated being an invalid."

"Despised it. The main reason I moved to San Francisco was because it was as far west of my tender loving relatives as I could get without falling into the Pacific. I needed to stand on my own two feet again—excuse the pun." Unable to bear the bittersweet feel of his touch for another moment, she reached down toward her rolled-up pajama leg.

Derek stopped her by catching her wrist and moving her hand firmly back to her lap, obviously intending to smooth the pajamas back into place himself. He grasped the soft fabric in both hands and began to unroll it, then stopped. Shooting a quick look up at her, he shocked her by leaning over to brush the gentlest of kisses across her kneecap. Her leg jumped reflexively. Without a word Derek finished rolling the pajama leg down, smoothed the fabric from knee to ankle with excruciating slowness, then released her. In an easy, gracefully coordinated movement he turned and sat beside her on the sofa, wincing when a semiprotruding spring poked him in the posterior. "Just where *are* your tender loving relatives?" he inquired as if he hadn't just caused her heart to leap into her throat and hang there in quivering convulsions. "Obviously you're from the south. Memphis?"

Summer blinked twice and swallowed her heart back into her chest, deciding to follow Derek's lead and ignore that odd little kiss. She'd have plenty of time to think about it later—and she knew she would think about it. When she spoke, her voice was amazingly normal. "Hasn't Connie told you anything about me? I just assumed you knew that I limped and where I'm from."

Derek shook his head, his expression grim. "We haven't talked much," he admitted. "Every time we try to have a conversation, we end up in a fight."

Summer decided not to mention that Connie had been rather more vocal with her roommate. Summer knew how disappointed Connie had been when her brother had moved back home after so many years only to treat her in very much the same heavily paternal manner that he would have shown her had she still been an adoring ten-year-old. Giving unwanted advice, criticizing her choice of jobs and lack of long-term career goals, reminding her that her impulsive nature and stubborn independence had led her into an ill-fated marriage before her eighteenth birthday. Expecting Derek to return to the States as a sophisticated, indulgent older brother with the heart of an adventurer and the fascinating stories of a seasoned world traveler, Connie had instead been faced with a determinedly conservative businessman, closemouthed about himself and intent on settling into a quietly successful routine.

Derek turned the conversation back to Summer before she had time to comment on his relationship with his sister. "All I know about you is that you've been rooming with Connie for eight months, that the two of you have a great deal in common, according to her, and that you both work in the accounting department of Pro Sporting Goods. You're, uh—" he paused, seeming to grope for the right words "—you're different than what I expected."

"In what way?" she asked curiously, wondering if his preconceptions of her had been as inaccurate as hers of him.

But he refused to enlighten her. "Just different," he replied unhelpfully. "I'd like to know more about you. So answer my question. Where are you from. Memphis?"

"You're close. I'm from Rose Bud, Arkansas."

He sighed. "Why do you insist on making fun of me when I'm only trying to talk to you? Where are you really from?"

Relieved at the change of mood, Summer laughed at him. "I told you. Rose Bud, Arkansas. Population two hundred and two. It's just down the road from Romance, about fifty-five miles north of Little Rock, if that pinpoints it for you."

"You're serious?"

"Yep. My parents own a seed and feed store there." She waited expectantly.

He groaned, thinking of her last name. "Not, er, Reed's Seed and Feed?"

She laughed again. "That's exactly what it's called. The store was nearly blown away by a big tornado a couple of years back that wiped out about half the buildings in Rose Bud—even the pool hall. But Dad got busy and rebuilt his place and most of the other merchants did the same, and now the town looks almost new. We even got us a red brick post office." She was chattering to mask her lingering nervousness, but Derek only listened, looking at her as if he weren't quite sure whether to believe a word of what she was telling him.

When he spoke, it was in a carefully neutral voice. "I like your laugh. It sounds like . . . like . . ."

"Like the tinkling of dozens of fairy bells?" she supplied helpfully.

"Certainly not," he retorted with a look of disgust that sent her laugh pealing through the room once again. "Who told you that?"

"A very handsome young man with aspirations of becoming a poet."

"Did he succeed?"

"Not so far. The last I heard, he was selling waterless cookware."

Again Derek shot her a suspicious look before asking another question. "Do you have any sisters or brothers?"

"Two sisters. Spring's a year older than I am—she's twenty-six. She's an optometrist living in Little Rock. Autumn's about to turn twenty-four. She's an electrician."

"An electrician? That's an unusual occupation for a young—Dammit, Summer, I told you to cut the bull! Do you honestly expect me to believe that your parents named their daughters Spring, Summer and Autumn? You've been feeding me a line all along, haven't you?" He glared at her as she rocked with laughter, her sore knee forgotten.

"Oh, Derek!" she gasped. "I love that look of outrage on your face. It's so cute. And now you look outraged and appalled. I love it!" Wiping at the tears of laughter that were making streaky paths through her faint mascara rings, she shook her head, trying to control her amusement. "I swear to you that every word I told you is true. I can't help it if my life sounds like one of those phony southern television programs—*The Dukes of Hazzard* or *Gomer Pyle U.S.M.C.* or something equally stupid. That was really the way I grew up."

"You really have a sister named Spring who's an optometrist and one named Autumn who's an electrician? And your father really does own a store called
Reed's Seed and Feed in Rose Bud, Arkansas?"

"I truly do and he truly does," she assured him,
making a determined effort not to laugh again. Really,
Derek could make some of the funniest faces. Connie
hadn't been exaggerating about that, even if she had
misled Summer by telling her that Derek was dull and
ordinary. Summer was finding out rapidly that nothing could be further from the truth.

Derek shook his head. "No wonder you and my sister are such good friends. At least it sounds as if you fit
in very well with your family. Connie swears *she* must
have been given to the wrong family at the hospital.
Neither my parents nor I could ever really figure her
out."

Summer sobered abruptly. "You're wrong about my
family. I never fit in, either. My parents might sound
like nuts, but they are staid, hardworking people with
very little imagination. Dad's store is called Reed's Seed
and Feed because that's his name and that's what he
sells. My sisters and I were named after the seasons of
our births—Spring's birthday's in May, mine's in July
and Autumn's is in September. My parents always
complained that I laughed at them from the day I was
born and they could never catch on to the joke. I love
them, of course, but honestly, they can be so exasperating."

"And your sisters? Are they dull and uptight like
me?" Derek inquired glumly. "Do you and Connie
make jokes about them, as well?"

Summer's hand fluttered in the air as she searched for
words to describe her sisters. "We're just different, that's

all," she said finally. "Spring's the brainy one, the one with all the ambition. She worked her way through college, then optometry school, and now she has opened a nice practice in Little Rock. She's quite serious, though she can be fun when she loosens up. She really has a cute sense of humor; she just keeps it well hidden. She reminds me a little of you, actually. Perhaps you should meet her, Derek. Did you say something?"

"No," he answered wryly. "Go on. Tell me about Autumn." He shifted a little closer on the worn couch, lazily, as if he were only interested in hearing more about her family. His leg brushed Summer's thigh, and she backed off immediately, then mentally scolded herself for bringing a knowing smile to his eyes.

"Autumn's the liberated one," she said a little breathlessly. "Fiercely independent, determined to prove herself equal to any man. It's her way of rebelling against the small-town Southern values that were pounded into all of us while we were growing up. You know, women exist only to serve men, a woman's greatest destiny is helpmate and mother, et cetera, et cetera. When she's not on her soapbox about the oppression of women, Autumn's okay. Spring disapproves of my lack of ambition, and Autumn thinks I'm a traitor to women because I believe in fairy tales, but we get along fine as long as we don't spend extended periods of time in one another's company."

"And what is Summer like?" Derek asked unexpectedly, his eyes keen behind the polished lenses of his glasses.

One slender shoulder lifted in a shrug. "I told you all about me last night. Remember? When I listed the reasons why I didn't fulfill your requirements for wife candidate." For some reason that little joke wasn't quite as amusing this morning, nor as easy to toss out.

"I remember everything you said to me last night," Derek answered, looking at her steadily. "Did you drop out of college because of your accident?"

"Yes. I dropped out not long before I probably would have flunked out, anyway."

"You don't seem to be lacking in intelligence."

"Thank you, sir. Actually, there were a few people who suggested that my college career might have been more profitable had I ever attended classes or opened a textbook. It was a novel idea, but I was creamed by the Ford before I ever had the opportunity to try it." When Derek just looked at her, she added, "That was a joke, Derek. I *did* attend a few classes, you know."

"I'm perfectly capable of recognizing a joke when I hear one," he informed her. He stood suddenly, reaching down a hand to help her up. "Get dressed. I'm taking you out for breakfast."

She looked surprised but accepted his assistance after only a momentary hesitation. "What am I, your surrogate sister?"

"Hell, no. I'm hungry and I don't care for eating alone."

"What a gracious invitation. Thank you, Derek, I'd love to have breakfast with you." She smiled brilliantly. As long as she could laugh at him, she could keep her disturbing attraction to him under control, she told herself optimistically.

He had the grace to look sheepish. "Sorry. I'm not usually so clumsy."

"I'm sure you're not," she told him kindly. "Working for the government for so long must have made you a master of civilized diplomacy. I guess I just have a talent for bringing out the worst in you."

Derek threw her a dark look and shoved his hands into his pockets. "Why is it that I always feel like I'm being insulted by you?"

She gave him a cheeky grin and patted his arm as she limped past him. "Because you're an astute and perceptive man, Derek Anderson. Give me twenty minutes to shower and change and I'll be ready to leave."

"I'll give you thirty," he offered magnanimously.

Reluctant to keep Derek waiting in the cluttered living room, Summer showered and washed her hair quickly. Her short, short hairdo took little time to style, and she applied only a minimum of makeup before pulling on her clothes. At random she selected a red, short-sleeved camp shirt to wear under a sleeveless yellow cotton vest. Her dirndl skirt of red-and-yellow plaid fell to midcalf, adequately concealing the ravages of her right knee. Sliding her feet into low-heeled red espadrilles, she was ready.

And then she wasted almost five minutes trying to tell herself that she was *not* on the verge of hyperventilating just because Derek Anderson was taking her to breakfast. What was it about him that made her turn into a swooning adolescent? she wondered with wry humor. What was it about his silvery eyes that made her long to see them glimmer with his smile? What was it about his strong arms that made her fantasize about having them around her? And how could one little kiss brushed lightly across her ugly, scarred knee turn her into a panting lapdog wanting only to feel his hands upon her? Disgusting, she told herself sternly, frowning at her image in the mirror.

But nice. There was something definitely nice about the feelings he brought out in her. Oh, she was going to have to be very careful.

As fast as she had been, Derek had been faster. Summer gasped when she stepped into the living room to find all the remains of last night's party cleared away. She found Derek in the kitchen, loading the last chip bowl into the dishwasher. A large plastic bag of garbage, neatly tied, rested at his feet. "Where do you take your garbage?" he asked, glancing up to find her staring at him.

"You wouldn't happen to be wearing a Superman costume under those mild-mannered businessman's clothes, would you?" she asked curiously.

His lips curved into one of his faint, dangerous smiles. "No. Would you like me to take them off and show you?"

*Yes.* The answer popped into her mind with such conviction that Summer blinked, telling herself that his occasional flashes of humor were definitely strange. "What I meant was," she enunciated clearly, "how did you ever get all this done so quickly?"

"Organization and efficiency." His eyes gleamed with that smile that so rarely touched his mouth. Summer was beginning to like that camouflaged smile very much. "I thought it was the least I could do after knocking you down when I arrived."

"It wasn't necessary, but thanks."

"You're welcome. You look very nice."

"Thank you again. We can leave now, unless you'd like to clean the bathroom first?"

She had injected just enough wistful hinting into the question to cause Derek's mouth to quirk into a genuine smile. "I think I'll pass on that opportunity."

Amazing what a mere curve of lips and a very brief glimpse of even white teeth could do for a rather ordinary male face, Summer thought in momentary bemusement. His rare smile made Derek look almost handsome. Downright sexy. And he was looking at her like . . .

"Breakfast," she said determinedly, shaking off her unsettling fascination with his facial expression and turning back toward the living room.

Derek chuckled and followed her, placing a warm palm on her back as they left her apartment. Summer tried very hard to ignore it. She failed completely.

# 3

DEREK TOOK HER to a restaurant in a nearby luxury hotel—a far cry from the quick Egg McMuffin that she
sometimes picked up on the way to work, if she ate
breakfast at all. He allowed her to make a good start on
her generous meal before asking about his sister. "Why
did she leave for Los Angeles at such an odd hour? And
what is she doing there?"

"It was an impulsive trip," Summer explained. "Do
you remember seeing Cody Pierce at the party last
night? Curly red hair, plaid sport coat?"

He frowned, remembering. "Yes."

"He has aspirations of becoming a stand-up comic.
Actually he's a systems analyst, but he's been performing at some local improv clubs, which led to a chance
to perform at The Comedy Store in L.A. tonight. He
mentioned last night that he was really nervous, and he
asked Connie to go along for moral support. She accepted, threw some things in an overnight bag, and they
left at midnight. For luck."

"For luck?" Derek repeated, looking confused.

"That's what they said," Summer answered cheerfully, reaching for her coffee. "Don't you ever do anything impulsive, Derek? Just for the fun of it?"

"Not very often," he answered flatly.

She nodded as if in perfect understanding. "I suppose it would be too dangerous in your former line of
work."

His brows drew sharply downward. "What?"

Her eyes wide and guileless, she replied, "Why, the spy business, of course. You weren't just teasing me about that, were you, Derek?"

"Oh, that." He drained his coffee cup. "What do you think?" he asked smoothly, setting his cup back on the table and eyeing her enigmatically. "*Was* I teasing you?"

She smiled. "I don't think you quite know how to tease, Derek." He did, of course. He'd teased her delightfully about having been a spy. Was that when she'd started to like him so much? Or had it been from the moment she'd set eyes on him?

"Maybe you should teach me," he suggested smoothly. "You seem to be an expert at it."

She only shrugged and smiled weakly, still wrestling with her own mental questions.

A waitress approached quietly to refill Derek's cup. Derek waited until the woman had left before asking, "Is Connie dating this Pierce guy?"

"She's been out with him a couple of times. She's not dating anyone seriously."

Derek looked grim as he pushed away his well-cleaned breakfast plate. "One of our cousins told me that Connie's been sleeping with anything in pants since her divorce. Is that true?"

Summer dropped her fork. "What a tacky thing to ask me! As if I'd tell you the intimate details of my best friend's love life. It must have been Barbara who made that catty remark to you. Connie's told me her cousin Barbara is a self-righteous snob."

Derek looked pained. "Barbara is a very respectable woman who has raised two exceptionally well-behaved daughters. She has been genuinely concerned about

Connie and was hoping I could exert my influence over my sister."

"Connie doesn't need your influence, Derek," Summer informed him flatly. "She's doing just fine. When you showed up this morning to take her to breakfast, I thought you were finally going to try to be her friend. But if you were only going to start lecturing her again, I'm glad she's out of town."

"I wasn't going to lecture her," he snapped irritably. "I was going to tell her I was sorry about the way we parted last night. Still, she needs someone to make her see that she's wasting her life: a dead-end job, endless parties, kooky friends and a dump of an apartment furnished with junk the Salvation Army would probably reject. What kind of life is that for an attractive young woman with Connie's intelligence?"

"I'm trying very hard not to take your incredibly arrogant and condescending remarks as a personal insult," Summer said, holding on to her temper with an effort. Strange, she fumed, she didn't usually have a problem with her temper. She usually found a reason to laugh when others got angry. But she could find very little humor in Derek Anderson's reference to Connie's "wasted life." Instead, she felt vaguely hurt and disappointed, as if he'd been talking about her rather than Connie. Had she been so foolish as to begin to hope that her attraction to Derek might lead to something more? If so, his words had shown her how silly that expectation had been. Summer had lived with disapproval for most of her life; she had no intention of getting involved with any man who could not accept her—or her friends—just as they were.

"If you'll remember, I work at the same dead-end job, I go to the same endless parties, I have the same kooky friends and I live in the same dump of an apartment furnished with the same Salvation Army rejects. And I'm perfectly content, thank you—even though I don't have an older, wiser brother to exert his influence on me. Thank God."

"I wasn't trying to criticize *you*, Summer," he said hastily, visibly uncomfortable. "What you do is your business. I just hate to see Connie, well—"

"You're only going to make it worse, Derek, so I think you'd better drop it," Summer told him, trying to sound cross though her irrepressible sense of humor was already diluting her unaccustomed anger, as it had so many times in the past. She rested her elbows on the polished tabletop and tapped her fingertips against her cheek, drawing on that comfortable humor. "Unless you want me to retaliate by telling you what I think of your life?"

"You don't know anything about the way I live," he informed her. "You've done nothing but poke fun at me and look down your up-tilted little nose at me since we met last night, simply because I wear conservative clothes and think there should be more to life than parties and games."

"And Connie and I think that life is short, so we should make every effort to enjoy it," Summer retorted, thinking of how easily her own life could have ended in that accident five years ago. How a shattered knee and equally shattered dreams could have led to a life of bitterness had she not resolved then to hang on to her humor and her sense of fun, no matter what else might befall her.

"Are you telling me that you enjoy the job you're in now?" Derek asked skeptically.

"I enjoy the paycheck very much, such as it is," she answered glibly. When he didn't reply, she prodded. "That was another joke, Derek. Should I cue you when to laugh?"

"I didn't find it particularly amusing," he replied. Actually, he'd been wondering what would happen if he tried to shut her smart little mouth with a kiss. He emptied his second cup of coffee, set the cup aside and straightened his glasses with a blunt fingertip. "I think we'd better talk about something else."

And *he'd* better keep reminding himself that this infuriatingly attractive young woman was off-limits, he added to himself grimly. There seemed to be little chance of her being equally attracted to a man she found so annoying and amusing. She'd made it pretty clear that he wasn't her type. Could he convince her that she was wrong? Did he want to try?

Talk about something else? Like what? Summer almost sighed, thinking of the many differences between them. One, in particular, was weighing on her mind. "Connie told me that you're a real sports enthusiast. She says you're quite a competitor. What types of sports do you enjoy, Derek?"

He shrugged, then realized that she was trying to make innocuous conversation and answered more fully. "I'm not quite as active as I used to be, but I still try to stay in shape. Working out bores me, so I get my exercise through participation in competitive sports. And I run every morning."

"Do you still run in marathons?"

Derek eyed her curiously. "Connie has told you a bit about me, hasn't she?"

Did he think his sister completely ignored her brother's existence? Summer wondered. "Of course she has, Derek. She talks about all of her family."

He looked thoughtful but answered her question. "I haven't run in a marathon since I came back to this country. I don't have the time to train properly since I've been so busy establishing my business."

"Do you miss it? Are you sorry you didn't become a professional athlete?"

"No. I'm doing exactly what I want to do. Sports are only a form of recreation for me. I get enough competition from the occasional tennis and racquetball game to satisfy my competitive urges." He smiled a little, knowing how Connie talked about him.

Summer toyed with her fork, remembering Connie had mentioned that Derek usually dated women who were as athletic as he was. According to his sister, a typical date with Derek usually consisted of working up a sweat on a tennis court. Connie had been sneering at the time, and Summer had laughed. She didn't find it quite so funny now that she'd actually met Derek. She thought of the woman Connie had most recently mentioned in connection with Derek.

"Connie tells me that you've been seeing Senator Payne's daughter since you've moved to Sausalito," she heard herself saying, surprised that she'd actually brought the subject up. "I met her at a party once. She's quite beautiful."

He lifted one eyebrow behind his glasses. "Yes, she is. I took her out a few times, but we're not seeing each other now."

Summer leaned both elbows on the table and rested her chin on her linked hands, gazing at him. "Why ever not?"

"Summer—"

"No, really, Derek, I would think she'd be exactly what you'd be looking for in a corporate wife." Her humor had resurfaced, for some strange reason, the moment he'd informed her that he was no longer seeing Joanne. She decided not to dwell on reasons as she continued to tease him.

"Summer, this is really none of your—"

Her face was all innocence when she interrupted him again. "After all, she's cultured, refined, educated, athletic. Exactly what you've tried to mold Connie into being. She has a career. I've seen her paintings, and they're quite interesting, though not exactly my style. Of course, she *is* thirty. Still, more and more women are having children after thirty these days."

"Summer?"

"Yes, Derek?"

"If I promise to stop criticizing the way you live, will you shut up?"

She laughed, inordinately pleased that the suggestion of a smile was back in his silvery-gray eyes.

"Why, yes, Derek, that sounds like a fair deal to me."

Derek kept a hand at her elbow as they left the restaurant soon afterward and walked to his tasteful gray Lincoln. A protective hand, Summer thought with resigned amusement. Of course he would be the type to want to assist the slender young woman with the bad limp—even if he *did* disapprove of her. So, as usual when something made her uncomfortable, she cracked a joke. "You know, with all its hills, San Francisco is a great place for me to live. I just keep my gimpy leg uphill and I walk almost straight. Of course, going the other direction is—"

"Don't do that," Derek cut her off sharply. "Don't make light of your injury."

Summer sighed. "Oops. I forgot to cue you again. It was a joke, Derek."

"It wasn't funny."

She sighed again, wishing once more that she wasn't so foolishly attracted to this man who seemed to disapprove of everything she did.

Derek hesitated before starting the car. "It's a beautiful day. Would you like to go for a drive with me, maybe take a stroll through Chinatown or visit Golden Gate Park?"

"Thank you, Derek, that sounds lovely, but I can't," Summer answered regretfully. "I have plans for today. I really should be getting back home."

She wondered if the brief flicker of expression that crossed his face was disappointment. She found herself hoping that it was.

At her door she thanked Derek politely for buying her breakfast and promised to have Connie call when she returned from Los Angeles the next day.

"Thanks." Derek stood awkwardly just inside the apartment. Why was he so reluctant to leave? he asked himself. What would she do if he were to kiss her? He'd been aching to taste her smile since the thought had occurred to him at breakfast. Even before that.

Summer wondered if she should offer him a cola or something. Derek seemed almost reluctant to leave, and to be honest, she wouldn't mind spending a little more time with him. She had about half an hour before Clay picked her up for their late-morning appointment at Halloran House. Giving in to temptation, she said, "Would you like to stay for a little while? We could . . . we could get to know each other a little better. After all, you are my best friend's brother."

"Summer—" Derek bit off whatever he'd been going to say, looked at her in silence for a long time, then reached out to touch her cheek. A butterfly touch that elicited a fluttery little response somewhere in the pit of her stomach. She stared at him, wide-eyed, as his head lowered very slowly. He was going to kiss her, she thought in startled wonder. Why? Did she really want him to?

*God, yes.*

She felt his breath on her parted lips. And then the telephone rang.

Derek jerked his head up and around, staring at the instrument as if he'd like very much for it to explode into oblivion. Feeling much the same way, Summer cleared her throat and limped to the end table where one of the apartment's extensions sat. "Hello?" she asked a little hoarsely. "When, tonight? Sure, that sounds like fun." She felt Derek move restlessly beside her. "Yeah, Clay's supposed to pick me up in about a half hour. I'll tell you about it tonight. See you at seven. Bye."

Derek looked particularly stern when she turned uncomfortably back to him. "Uh, Derek—Well, darn," she muttered as the telephone rang again. She looked at him apologetically.

"Look, I'd better go. I'll see you later, okay?" Derek ground out, heading for the door. She had men standing in line for her, he told himself angrily. Damn.

Her hand on the telephone receiver, Summer swallowed a sigh. "All right. Thanks for breakfast, Derek."

He only nodded as he walked out of the apartment. Summer picked up the telephone, explained that Connie wasn't home, promised to relay a message and hung up.

Chewing on her lower lip, she walked into her bedroom, thinking that her impromptu breakfast date with Derek had been unexpectedly nice. They got along quite well when they weren't talking about Connie. Or Summer's limp. She wondered why her self-directed jokes bothered him so much. Most people thought the comments were funny and admired her for being able to laugh at life's misfortunes. Obviously, seeing her scars had bothered Derek so much that he didn't even want to discuss them. Her hand went unconsciously to her knee. Derek wasn't the first man who'd been turned off by her scars and her limp, she reflected grimly.

She tried to divert her thoughts by remembering how easily she and Derek had conversed, almost like old friends. Then she told herself that he would probably have even more to talk about with a woman like Joanne Payne, the senator's lovely daughter. The thought made her feel depressed again.

As she gathered the things she would take with her to Halloran House, she tried to tell herself that she couldn't care less whom Derek dated. There was certainly nothing between Summer and Derek, other than their mutual involvement with Connie. Perhaps he was a little attracted to her, as she was to him, but that was all there was to it.

"It's just that I think Connie's wrong about Derek," she told the enormous Winnie the Pooh bear that sat beside her bed. "He's a pretty nice guy, even if he *is* a little stuffy and arrogant, and all he needs is to fall madly in love with someone who'd keep that lovely smile in his eyes."

Now what had put that thought into her head? "I wasn't talking about myself, of course," she assured the sympathetic bear, patting his one-eared head, her fingers lingering on the heavy stitches that repaired the gash where his other ear had once been. "I'm waiting for a hero, remember? Derek might *look* kind of heroish, but he's just too...too proper. He'd...he'd probably bore me to tears inside a week." Now why didn't she have more conviction in her voice?

And why were her thoughts lingering on the brush of his lips against her scarred knee and the look in his eyes as he'd been so close to kissing her just before the telephone had interrupted? She wondered if she felt relieved or disappointed that the phone had stopped that unwise move.

Disappointed. Definitely disappointed.

SUMMER HAD CONSIDERED going to church Sunday morning, but for some reason she hadn't been able to go to sleep until very late the night before and she overslept. In an attempt to lighten her mood, which was rarely that gloomy, she turned on her radio and dressed in a bright purple sweatshirt and her most comfortable jeans. By early afternoon she had thoroughly cleaned the apartment and was restlessly trying to think of what she wanted to do for the remainder of the day. She could call a friend and go shopping, or there was a barbecue that she'd been invited to attend. She'd gone to a movie and then out for drinks with two women friends the night before—it had been that invitation that had interrupted yesterday when Derek had been about to kiss her—and her friends had assured her that the barbecue party would be "crawling with hunks." So why didn't she want to go? She dropped onto the couch and rested her chin in her hands, wondering why none of her usual pastimes held any appeal for her that day. When the telephone rang, she lifted the receiver with a spark of optimism, hopeful that the call would provide the answer to her boredom. "Hello?"

"Summer, it's Derek."

"Derek!" She wondered at her sudden surge of excitement, then scolded herself as she realized why he was calling. "Sorry, Connie's not back yet. She probably won't be home until late."

"I wasn't calling to talk to Connie," Derek replied unexpectedly. "I wondered if you have plans for the afternoon."

"I was just trying to decide. Why?"

"Would you like to come to my house for a swim? We can throw some steaks on the grill afterward for dinner. I'd like to talk to you about Connie."

Her initial pleasure at the invitation evaporated with his explanation. "I thought I'd made myself clear about the subject of Connie, Derek. I like her, I think she's getting along fine and I refuse to help you interfere in her life."

Derek's sharp exhalation was clearly audible through the telephone line. "Summer, I'm not asking you to help me interfere in her life. Connie's my sister, and I'm tired of feeling like there's a war going on between us. You're her best friend, so I thought maybe you could help me find a way to make peace with her."

"The only way you're going to be able to do that is to accept her just as she is," Summer answered bluntly.

"I'll try. Will you come over and give me some pointers?"

She wiggled her bare feet on the coffee table in front of her and watched them with a little smile playing at the corners of her mouth. "How are you at taking advice, Derek?"

"I haven't had a great deal of experience at it," he answered ruefully, "but I can try. Shall I pick you up in an hour?"

"Sure. See you then." She hung up the phone and wriggled her toes happily. She tried to tell herself that she was suddenly in such a good mood because she now had plans for the rest of the day. She tried to tell herself that she was pleased that Derek seemed willing to try to patch things up with his sister, which should make both Anderson siblings happier. But she knew that the real reason she felt good was that she would be spending the afternoon in the company of a man she was beginning to like very much. Not an ideal hero, of course, she reminded herself rather sternly, trying to quell some of the anticipation she felt toward seeing him with her old, standard excuse for not getting involved. Still, teasing Derek had turned out to be more fun than she'd expected.

Then her smile faded. Swimming. She'd have to wear a bathing suit in front of him. Her body wasn't so bad, but there was no way to conceal her mutilated right knee in a swimsuit. After five years she'd learned to wear her maillots and occasional shorts without too much regard for what others thought of her scars, but for some reason Derek's reaction was more important to her. She told herself that she was being silly. He'd already seen the scars, hadn't he? Still, she knew that her scars and limp would only remind both of them of the many reasons there could be nothing more between Summer and Derek than friendship. He would want a woman who was more nearly perfect, physically and every other way. Summer wanted a man who could accept her, flaws and all.

So she would concentrate on making friends with him and helping him do the same with his estranged sister. And she would try very hard to avoid any more intimate scenes like that near kiss the morning before. No matter how much she might be tempted to do otherwise.

IN HIS ELEGANT SAUSALITO HOME Derek replaced his own receiver and frowned down at the telephone beneath his hand. Calling Summer with the impromptu invitation had been an impulse, just as dropping by to invite his sister to breakfast yesterday had been. Dumb move, Anderson, he told himself.

He wondered dispassionately at the urge that had made him call Summer and invite her to his home. True, he wanted very much to come to some kind of an understanding with Connie. And true, Summer was Connie's best friend and would therefore be the logical person to advise him on how best to approach Connie with a long-overdue attempt at reconciliation. But was that really the reason he'd called Summer? Or was it just an excuse to spend more time with her?

From the little Connie had told him about her roommate, he hadn't expected to like Summer Reed immediately. But he had. So much so that he'd wanted to spend more time with her. Alone. He had to ask himself if the real reason he'd wanted to ask Connie to breakfast yesterday had been so that he could see Summer again and find out if she was really as intriguing as she'd seemed at the party. She was.

He swallowed, remembering the rush of heat that had hit him at her door. He wanted to be with Summer, not only because she made him want her to the point of distraction but also because she had proved to be such damned good company. She irritated him, she amused him, she kept him on his toes. She made him feel alive again, really alive for the first time in nearly a year. He'd thought he was past thriving on risks and challenges. It seemed that he was not.

Summer was not at all the type of woman he'd expected to find himself suddenly obsessed with. And yet he was.

It was a shame she was wasting her very obvious intelligence and competence in a job that admittedly bored her and a series of parties that seemed only to fill her free hours. Of course, he had no right to criticize her. Could it be that his sister's life should be equally exempt from his well-meant interference?

He had never meant to drive Connie away from him when he'd come home. It was just that he'd had such expectations for her when she'd been a bright, spunky little girl. He couldn't help but be disappointed that she wasn't taking advantage of the opportunities she'd had to better herself. Ever since her marriage to that jerk actor when she'd been no more than a kid, she'd seemed intent on living as frivolously as possible. Was he supposed to just stand by and say nothing?

With a frown and a shake of his head he abandoned the troublesome self-debate and allowed himself—just for a moment—to contemplate Summer's visit with an unfamiliar sense of anticipation.

Catching sight of himself in a mirror on the wall in front of him, he realized he was wearing a stupid, infatuated schoolboy grin. The expression made him look like a stranger, even to himself. What was this woman doing to him to make him look like that? What was it about her that was tying him in knots, making him plot and connive for ways to convince her to spend more time with him?

He was going to have to be very careful, he told himself sternly, the grin slowly fading to be replaced by a look of wary caution.

And then he found himself whistling as he started toward his kitchen to thaw the steaks.

"YOU'RE AN EXCELLENT SWIMMER," Derek complimented Summer after a swimming race he'd won only
with great effort.

Gasping for breath, Summer clung to the edge of the
pool, tossing her wet bangs out of her eyes and smiling
at him. "Thanks," she said when she'd regained her
voice. "I spent hours in pools during my recuperation
from my accident to strengthen my leg. I still try to
swim laps three or four times a week."

Derek reached out to brush a wet strand of hair away
from her eyes. "I thought you said you weren't athletic."

She wanted to turn her cheek into his hand, to drop
a kiss into his palm. Instead, she casually shook his
hand away and pulled herself out of the pool. "I'm not,"
she threw back at him, reaching for her gaily colored
beach towel. "Exercising is just something I do, or I'd
end up walking more like a duck than I do now."
Wrapping herself in the huge towel, she dropped onto
a lounge chair at the pool's edge, watching as Derek
shoved himself out of the rippling blue water.

More than once during the afternoon she'd found
herself tempted to ignore her resolution to keep things
between them strictly platonic. There had been several
incidents in the pool, when wet skin had brushed wet
skin, that could have turned into something dangerous if both she and Derek hadn't been so obviously

trying to remain in control. She'd known from the moment he'd picked her up that Derek was as determined as she to make an effort to ignore the unbidden attraction that had flared between them from the beginning.

Summer had fallen instantly in love with Derek's home, a good-sized house of rock, cedar and smoked glass nestled into the Sausalito hills. Though she was sure the place had been professionally decorated, Derek had opted for comfort and warmth rather than trendy style. Each room he led her into on the quick tour he'd given her upon their arrival had been beautiful, yet Summer could easily imagine a family living in the home without worrying about smudges and clutter. She could be very comfortable in such a house, she found herself thinking, then made herself stop picturing herself in residence here. Such thoughts were detrimental to her peace of mind.

She'd been in Derek's company for more than two hours now and was surprised at how well they got along. Carefully avoiding the subject of his sister, they'd kept their conversation light and impersonal, with Summer tossing out her usual quota of one-liners and Derek serving with amiable resignation as her straight man. She had yet to make him laugh outright, but the hint of a smile had flashed frequently in his pewter-gray eyes. The only quips that made him frown were the ones she made about her physical impairment.

In response to her remark about walking like a duck, he was scowling now as he draped his lean form on the chair beside his guest's. He pointedly made no reply.

Chuckling under her breath, Summer slid an oversize pair of purple-framed sunglasses onto her nose and settled comfortably in her chair to enjoy the still-warm early September sun, allowing the beach towel to fall aside to reveal her becomingly simple scarlet maillot. It was simply habit to keep the towel draped over her scarred knee when she was with people she didn't know well. She was hardly aware that she had done so this time.

Derek was lounging in a position almost identical to her own, his eyes half closed as he squinted meditatively across the pool. Since he wasn't wearing his glasses, his eyes looked smaller, his dark lashes longer. Summer took advantage of the opportunity to study his roughly carved profile and powerful, slim physique.

When he had stripped to his conservative navy swim trunks, she'd realized that her first impression at the party Friday night had been correct. His body was as solid and firm as she'd first thought, corded with hard-earned muscles and marred only by an interestingly jagged scar across his left shoulder. Thinking of their silly repartee on the night they'd met, Summer mused that Derek's body looked like that of an ex-spy's, even if his sister would have scoffed at the very idea that he could do something so daring and irresponsible.

It had been easier than she'd expected to appear before him in her own swimwear. Though his eyes had drifted down to her scarred leg, he'd managed to keep any distaste he might have felt well hidden. He neither stared at the scars nor pointedly avoided them. Funny, she'd almost forgotten her earlier misgivings.

"Why are you keeping your right leg covered with your towel?" Derek asked suddenly, as if he'd read her mind.

Summer flushed a little and looked down. "Just habit, I guess."

"Obviously you don't always keep it covered or your right leg wouldn't be as tanned as your left," Derek pointed out logically. "Your scars don't bother me, Summer. I have a few of my own, and I'm not trying to hide them."

Summer sighed and brushed the towel away from her knee. "You're right, of course. It's silly." She glanced at his shoulder. "How did you get yours?"

"Trying to prove what a hotshot jock I am," he answered, telling her nothing yet reminding her that this was a man who enjoyed sports of all kinds. Sports she would never be able to share with him, she told herself rather cruelly.

"Where were you attending college when you had your accident?" he asked suddenly.

Grateful for the distraction of Derek's question, Summer answered. "UALR—the University of Arkansas at Little Rock."

"What was your major?"

"Theater arts."

His eyebrow lifted. "Drama?"

"Mmm. Drama, dance, music."

"Had you had any training before you entered college?"

"Yes. I took dance lessons from the time I was three years old, after one of my aunts—a frustrated ballerina—decided I showed some talent. I loved it, and though my parents thought it was basically a waste of time, they never complained about the expense involved."

"What were you planning to do when you graduated?"

Summer fluffed her drying bangs with her fingertips and answered lightly. "Oh, I had dreams of becoming the next Mary Martin or Debbie Reynolds. I thought Hollywood would revive the musical comedy movies just for me."

"Were you any good?"

"Oi was bloomin' marv'lous, oi was," she answered in a shrill Cockney accent.

Derek nodded approvingly. "You played Eliza Doolittle?"

"I beat out two dozen others for the spring production of *My Fair Lady* my sophomore year. Which was rather surprising since I only auditioned to please my boyfriend, a gorgeous senior who'd won the part of 'Enry 'Iggins."

Derek frowned at the mention of her old boyfriend but let it pass without comment. Still, he had more questions to ask. "How were your reviews?"

She sighed dramatically. "Alas, I'll never know. I was on my way to the final dress rehearsal when I had the close encounter with the motorcycle-eating Ford. My stand-in got all the rave reviews." Summer had gotten drugs to dull the agonizing pain in her shattered knee, and the news that she would never dance on stage again.

Derek sat still for a moment, studying her seemingly unregretful expression before finally asking, "Whatever happened to 'Enry 'Iggins?"

"As soon as he graduated, he headed for the bright lights of New York. He's on a daytime soap now."

"Do you ever hear from him?"

"No. He married an actress on the same soap. We broke up soon after my accident." And she'd learned that active men did not want to be slowed down by a woman with a handicap. She'd do well to keep that in mind now, she told herself.

"Was he a hero-type?"

Summer forced a laugh. "Hardly. He took one look at my mangled leg in the hospital and fainted dead away. He managed to visit me twice before he announced that he just couldn't deal with it and took off for New York. The really funny part is that he plays a doctor on the soap."

"You don't appear to be brokenhearted."

She shrugged. "It's ancient history." And broken hearts mend with time, as do broken limbs, though the scars remain for a lifetime.

"You told me that you've had several jobs since you left college. What have you done, and how did you end up in the accounting department of Pro Sporting Goods?"

"What is this, an interview?"

"You interest me. I'd like to know more about you," Derek replied candidly. "You don't have to answer if you don't want to."

"What the heck. Somehow you've managed to drag my entire life story out of me during the two times we've been together. You might as well ask about my work history, too." She shoved her sunglasses higher on her nose. "While I was recovering from the accident, I kept the books for my father's store. We were both relieved when I ditched the walker and decided to look for employment in Little Rock. There I found a job in a small credit union for a while, but it was so boring. I quit after only four months."

"Then what?"

"Well, my next job was in a ladies' dress shop, but it didn't work out."

He groaned. "Let me guess. You told the ladies exactly how they looked in the dresses they tried on."

She giggled. "How did you know? That's exactly what I did. Can you imagine how some of those, um, well-endowed women looked in dresses two sizes too small and ten years too young? I could tell I wasn't cut out to be a saleswoman, so I decided to move here and try something new."

"Why San Francisco?"

"I had a crush on Michael Douglas when I was a teenager. I watched *The Streets of San Francisco* every week, so when I decided to get out of Arkansas and started imagining all the places I could go, I automatically thought of San Francisco."

"That's a damned odd way to choose a place to pick up and move to," Derek grunted, looking at her again with that dull silver glint that told her he wasn't quite sure whether she was teasing him.

"A lot of things I do are damned odd," she replied airily.

"I wondered if you were aware of that."

"But fun," she added, swinging her legs over the side of the lounge chair. "Any further questions?" she asked as she sat up facing him.

"How many jobs have you had here?"

"Only two. The first was as a hostess in a lovely little restaurant. That didn't work out, either."

"I'm almost afraid to ask why."

"Well, every time I invited the diners to 'walk this way'—"

"Summer, that's enough of the jokes about your limp. It's sick humor, and I don't find it at all amusing."

"It's called gallows humor, and you're just too stuffy to appreciate it."

He sighed but asked one final question. "How'd you get the job with Pro Sporting Goods?"

"No one else wanted it." She stood, dropping her towel. "If the inquisition's over, I'm going back into the pool."

He waved a hand to indicate that she could do as she liked, then watched broodingly as she limped to the side of the pool and dived expertly into the cool depths. In the water her awkwardness vanished, giving way to a graceful style that was a pleasure to watch. His eyes followed her through several laps, noting the racer's turns at the ends of the pool, modified so that she was pushing off only with her strong leg. Summer was a puzzle to him. She seemed too bright, too complex, to explain her apparently shallow approach to life. But when she'd told him about her accident and the long months of recovery, the end of her career as a dancer and as a performer, the desertion of her college boyfriend and the chain of unfulfilling jobs, she'd tossed out the pieces of information as if she'd been speaking of someone else. Did she really think that her glib manner hid the pain and traces of bitterness in her eyes? Was he the only one who could see them there?

Why the hell should he care? he asked himself exasperatedly. He barely knew the woman. She was someone he was spending time with only because he wanted her to help him get closer to his sister.

Bull. Even he didn't believe that.

He narrowed his eyes as Summer stopped swimming to float lazily on her back, her eyes closed in pleasure. Her trim, sleek figure floated effortlessly in the clear water. The wet scarlet maillot hugged her taut curves caressingly. Caressingly? Now where had that word come from? His palms were itching, but that didn't necessarily mean that he was imagining the feel of Summer's skin beneath them. Dammit, he had no intention of giving in to an inexplicable attraction to a woman who would only laugh at him if he should tell her how he felt. She probably used men as unconscionably as his sister, her alleged search for the perfect hero an excuse for going through scores of potential candidates. Someone could get hurt in a relationship with the flighty young woman in his pool—and chances were it wouldn't be Summer, he told himself sternly.

He closed his eyes and tried to remember if his palms had itched even once during his pleasantly uneventful, short-term affair with Joanne Payne. He didn't remember them doing so. Damn.

The steaks were tender and perfectly grilled, the weather beautiful for eating on the terrace overlooking his pool. Everything should have been fine, yet Derek realized that things had been going downhill between him and Summer since he'd questioned her so intensely an hour or so earlier. The lazily amused friendliness she had shown him during their swim had been replaced by an unsubtle mocking attitude that he was finding increasingly annoying. She'd gibed at him throughout the meal, making fun of his life-style, his bureaucratic establishment background, even his home. And all the while she looked so temptingly touchable as she lounged across the small patio table from him that he found himself wanting to haul her inside and throw himself on her slender body—after he warmed her fanny for daring to laugh at him.

He asked himself what he'd done to cause such an abrupt change in her manner toward him, then decided that he'd gotten too close with his questions. This was her way of paying him back for digging into history and emotions that she preferred to keep hidden behind her brilliant smile

He watched broodingly as she brushed her almost dry bangs back from her face in what he assumed was an unconsciously sexy gesture and widened those deceptively innocent blue eyes at him. "What's the matter, Derek? Something wrong with your steak?"

"No, it's fine," he answered shortly, glaring down at the expensive piece of meat that had lost its taste for him.

"Of course. You're very good with a grill. But then, you're very good at everything you do, aren't you, Derek? It must be nice to be so capable."

She made the word sound like a curse, Derek fumed, looking resentfully at her. He could feel himself going on the defensive, and he didn't like it. "I never claimed to be perfect, Summer."

"Didn't you?" Without giving him a chance to respond to her murmured question, she turned her head and looked slowly around the lovely lawn of his home. "Such a beautiful place. Did you have Joanne in mind when you bought this house?" she inquired blandly.

"Of course not," he answered impatiently, feeling his face grow hard with his rising anger. He breathed deeply, telling himself that she was using one of his sister's tricks of getting him mad so that he would do or say something she could pounce on to mock him further. "I bought the house because I like it and it's a good investment," he added in a determinedly even tone.

"Still, it looks like a family home. You must have had marriage in mind when you purchased it. If Joanne doesn't quite meet your requirements, perhaps Connie and I could find you someone else. I personally know several cultured, refined ladies that I would be happy to introduce you to. Of course, you'd better tell me what was wrong with Joanne so I'll know what to avoid when I set you up with someone."

Derek very deliberately set his napkin on the table beside his plate. "Drop it, Summer."

She eyed the set of his jaw. "It's not that I don't think you're capable of finding your own perfect mate," she assured him briskly. "I'm just trying to offer advice."

Enough was enough. Derek decided it was definitely time for him to regain control of this situation.

She hadn't seen him move. One minute he was sitting across the table glaring at her and the next he was standing beside her chair, having hauled her to her feet, holding her there with a biting grip on her upper arms. "Is this what it takes to shut you up?" he demanded gruffly, moments before his mouth covered hers.

The gasp that couldn't escape her lips lodged in her throat. Summer stood motionless in Derek's arms, too surprised to struggle against the angry embrace.

Actually, the bruisingly punishing kiss wasn't bad. Feeling his tongue thrusting inside to dominate her mouth, she responded tentatively, telling herself that it was only wise to humor an outraged male until he recovered his self-control. After all, it *was* her fault, sort of. And the only reason she allowed her arms to slide up and around his neck was that the sooner he was mollified, the sooner the kiss would end.

For all she knew, it could have been hours before Derek slowly lifted his mouth from hers. Sometime during the kiss the earth seemed to have tilted on its axis or something, leaving everything looking decidedly different to Summer's dazed, unfocused eyes. Even Derek's glasses looked crooked, which couldn't be the result of unrestrained passion—could it?

She thought she saw his fingers shaking a little when he reached up to straighten the dark frames but told herself that that, too, must be the result of her bemusement from the unexpectedly hypnotic kiss. "Uh, Derek—" she began tentatively, only to have him step away from her and cut her off with a sharp statement.

"Forget it, Summer."

She frowned. "What?"

"I know you find me vastly amusing and that you have thoroughly enjoyed your game of Derek-baiting during our meal, but it's going to stop right here. I'm not going to be the latest toy for your amusement."

"I don't know what you're talking about."

"The hell you don't," he returned roughly. "You told me at the party the other night that I wasn't your type and that you had no intention of becoming involved with someone like me, so all I can assume is that you've decided to entertain yourself with me. Am I that much of a novelty to you, Summer? Do you plan to laugh with Connie about how you seduced her straitlaced brother?"

"Hey!" she exclaimed abruptly. "Who kissed whom? *I* wasn't the one who initiated that little interlude."

"Do you deny that you provoked it?" he demanded.

*Had* she provoked it? Well, yes, she supposed she had, she admitted to herself, looking away from him for a moment. She'd been irresistibly tempted to try to shake that cool composure of his, but she'd impudently expected him to yell or kick something—preferably not her. "I suppose I did provoke you," she muttered. "I wanted to make you mad, but I never expected you to demonstrate your anger in quite that way."

Derek looked taken aback when she shot a quick look at him through her lashes. "You wanted to make me angry?"

"Yes."

"Why?"

"I was teaching you an object lesson," she told him, defiantly lifting her chin.

Derek cleared his throat and pulled at the neckline of his light blue T-shirt as if he were wearing a tie that had been knotted too tightly. "What kind of an object lesson?" he asked, forming the words with exaggerated care.

"I was trying to show you how infuriating it is for someone to interfere with your life. Who you date and why is none of my business, and you were quite correct to be annoyed by my nosy questions and comments—just as Connie has a right to be angry when you ask if she's 'sleeping with anything in pants,' as you put it. And just as I was irritated when you asked all those questions about my past and my job history, then looked so stuffy and disapproving when I answered you."

Derek leaned against the railing of the cedar deck, a thoughtful frown darkening his face. The view of the Golden Gate Bridge and its San Francisco skyline backdrop behind him was breathtakingly beautiful. But he was oblivious to the glory of his surroundings as he stared at the woman who faced him from a few feet away, her vivid blue eyes returning his look without blinking. "I think you made your point," he conceded after a time.

"Sorry about the way I went about it, but you just wouldn't listen when Connie or I tried to explain reasonably," Summer answered, straightening the red

Mexican gauze sundress she'd donned over her swim-suit as she offered a tentative truce with her tone.

Derek slowly shook his head. "You made me fu-rious," he told her softly.

She smiled faintly, still a little shell-shocked from his expression of that fury. "I know. Now you know how Connie feels when you start telling her how she ought to live and offering unwanted assistance."

For only a moment an expression of pain crossed Derek's tanned face. He turned to look out over the distant landscape, but not before Summer had seen the emotion and recognized it. She wondered if anyone else would have seen it, or whether she had become so at-tuned to Derek's feelings that she was almost psychic where he was concerned. She was unaware that her thoughts closely echoed the questions he had asked himself earlier about his ability to read her. Pushing her fanciful thoughts aside, she stepped closer to him and rested a small hand on his rigid arm. "Derek, it's not too late. You and Connie can still be friends, if you'd just give each other a chance. You have to accept her as she is, and she needs to learn that you're not really a hu-morless stuffed shirt."

He shot her a quick glance. "You don't think I am?"

"No," she answered ruefully, her most charming smile curving her unpainted mouth. "I think you're a pretty nice guy, actually. I mean, you *are* a stuffed shirt, but you're not a completely humorless stuffed shirt."

He chuckled—he actually chuckled! she thought in wonder—and then forgot to be pleased when he reached for her.

"Summer."

She stepped back so hastily that she had to clutch at the railing to maintain her precarious balance. "No,

Derek. No more of that. Whatever attraction the two of us might feel for each other could only lead to homicide. Possibly double homicide. I think we'd better stick to being friends."

Her logical little speech did not seem to accomplish the purpose she had intended. Derek's eyes narrowed thoughtfully behind his glasses. "You're attracted to me?" he asked with apparent intrigue.

She gulped and attempted an answer. "Well, yes, but—No, don't!" She wasn't quite quick enough this time to evade his reaching hands. She found herself plastered against his broad chest. "Oh, Derek, this isn't wise." She sighed, even as her head tilted back to welcome his kiss.

"No," he breathed against her moist, parted lips. "Not wise at all." And then his mouth covered hers.

This time the kiss was anything but punishing. In fact, Summer wondered dazedly if she were being rewarded for doing something wonderful. If kisses could be bronzed and hung on a wall for posterity, this one should be.

She lifted her arms and curled them around his neck, her fingers seeking the short hair at the nape of his neck. His hair felt so soft, so thick, his body so solid, so hard against hers. And growing harder.

"Oh, God, Summer," he groaned, slanting his head only to kiss her from a new angle. He slid his hands under the curves of her bottom, lifting her into his pelvis to show her quite graphically that the kiss was as powerful for him as it was for her. Summer could only moan softly and press closer. Her swimsuit and thin dress became unwanted barriers between them, as were his T-shirt and swim trunks. The warmth that penetrated their clothing taunted her, making her want even more.

When the second knee-melting kiss ended, Summer somehow found the strength to break away from him. Or maybe he'd decided to release her. Whatever it was, she stood panting for breath and staring at him in a kind of awed wariness that twisted his mouth into his infrequent smile. "Don't look at me like that, Summer," he ordered indulgently. "I was only teaching you an object lesson."

"An . . . an object lesson?" she asked in a breathless voice that showed an annoying tendency to squeak. "What object lesson?" she demanded, bringing her voice sternly under control.

He crossed his arms across his wide chest, looking rather pleased with himself, and leaned against the railing. "That people who teach object lessons sometimes get unexpected results," he replied quietly.

Summer blew her bangs out of her eyes and doubled her fists on her slender hips. "Look, Derek Anderson, if you and I are going to be friends—and I have serious doubts about whether that's possible—we're going to have to get something straight right now. I am *not* looking for an amusing toy to keep me entertained. I have no intention of getting involved with any man at this time, and especially not a proper, respectable businessman like you, even if you *are* an Olympic-class kisser. So let's forget this ever happened and make sure that it never happens again. Agreed?"

"Olympic-class, huh?" Derek looked disgustingly pleased with her ill-chosen adjective.

She sighed. "We were discussing your sister," she reminded him archly.

"So we were," he agreed, obviously deciding to allow her to lead the conversation—for now. "Let's carry these dishes inside and we can continue this discussion—about Connie—in the den."

# 5

"ABOUT CONNIE," Summer began when she and Derek had settled down with drinks in the den. She felt the need to say something since he continued to look at her in a way that made her rather nervous—as if he were ready for dessert and she were it.

"Yes?"

"D'you really think you'll be able to be her friend?"

"I can only try. Actually, I had an idea for a peace offering."

"Really? What?"

"I'm having a small cocktail party here next Saturday evening, one of those obligatory functions for my clients and potential clients. Do you think Connie would like to serve as my hostess?"

"I don't know, but you could ask her," Summer replied, pleased with the idea. "I think she'll be honored. It will make her feel like you trust her to behave herself in front of your associates."

"Can I trust her?"

"Of course you can! She knows how to act at a genteel cocktail party. She doesn't particularly like them, of course, but she would probably attend this one for your sake."

He nodded. "I'll ask her, then."

"Good." She smiled at him.

Derek shifted his weight, ending up a little closer to her on the deep, oatmeal-colored couch. Summer looked at him suspiciously, but he only said, "I'd like for you to come, too."

"Why?"

He lifted one eyebrow. "As Connie's friend, your being here might put her more at ease."

"Oh." For a moment she'd thought he was asking her simply because he wanted her to be there. She tried to tell herself that she wasn't disappointed that he was only thinking of Connie.

"Besides," he continued as if her thoughts had been audible to him, "I'd like for you to be here."

"Why?" she asked again.

"Because I enjoy your company," he replied simply.

"You do?"

"Yeah. I do." He leaned closer.

Summer backed off quickly. "I thought we'd agreed there would be no more of that."

"You agreed," he reminded her. "I agreed to no such thing."

She glared at him, trying to read his expression. Was he teasing her? The funny little smile was gleaming in his metallic eyes, but he didn't actually look as if he were teasing as he leaned even closer.

"Derek?"

"Yes, Summer?"

Intrigued by the way he'd said her name, she almost forgot what she'd been about to say. Then she remembered. "You don't approve of the way I live my life."

"Not entirely, no."

"And you're no hero."

"God, no."

"So it would be a waste of time for us to . . . you know."

"Perhaps."

"And you don't believe in wasting time, remember? Connie says—"

"Connie has a big mouth."

"I'm her best friend. She tells me everything." Then she remembered that she'd been about to make a point. "So do you agree that it would be best for us to remain friends?"

"You and Connie? Absolutely."

Summer growled. "No, Derek. You and I. *We* should remain friends. Nothing more."

"Yes, we probably should."

She relaxed. "Good. I'm glad that's settled." Now she had only to convince herself, she thought.

"So am I." He moved the six inches that separated them and kissed her deeply.

Her heart playing hopscotch in her throat, Summer stared at him when he pulled back. "Derek, haven't you been listening to a word I said?" she demanded. "You just agreed that we would remain friends. Friends don't sit around kissing each other."

"They don't?"

"Not . . . not the way you kiss."

"Olympic-class?" He still seemed rather pleased with that description.

"Well, actually, I think I should change that."

He looked disappointed. "Not Olympic-class?"

"No. I'd forgotten that all the competitors in the Olympics are amateurs. I don't think you'd qualify."

He grinned. It was the closest thing to a real grin she'd ever seen him wear. Before she could do any more than go all gooey inside in response, he was kissing her again. "You have the nicest way of asking a man to back off," he informed her when he released her mouth, keeping his face close to hers.

She cleared her throat with difficulty. "I don't think you're paying much attention."

"I don't seem to be, do I?"

Setting her half-empty wineglass pointedly on the low coffee table in front of them, Summer rose to her feet. "It's time for you to take me home now, Derek."

"All right," he agreed, standing beside her. "Will you come to my party next weekend? It's only fair, you know. I went to yours."

"I'll think about it."

"Do that."

DEREK FOUND HIMSELF actually smiling into the darkness as he climbed into bed that night. He'd stumbled onto an excellent way of dealing with Summer Reed, he decided in satisfaction. He'd wondered the other day what would happen if he silenced her teasing with a kiss. Now he knew. At first he'd merely been punishing her for her pointed little "object lesson." Then, when he'd discovered that his kisses seemed to shake her up so much that she actually forgot to laugh at him, he'd decided to continue the interesting assault. And face it, he told himself, he'd been wanting to kiss her ever since he'd first seen her sitting on that bar stool in her apartment, her lovely smile seeming to light up the dim corner in which she sat. She'd been so self-assured. So coolly amused.

Remembering her dazed expression when he'd left her at the door tonight with a kiss that could have blown all the fuses in her apartment building, he chuckled softly. He'd wondered if there was a way to penetrate her laughing composure. It seemed he had found it.

There was only one problem with his method of controlling Summer. He liked it too much. Kissing Summer could rapidly become addictive. It compared easily with the adrenaline rush that had come just before he'd gone into situations in his government work that he'd known would be highly dangerous. He could imagine only one thing more exciting than kissing her. Imagining that one thing had sent him straight home to a cold shower.

He thought of those dangerous situations that he'd faced with appalling regularity before he'd retired from the job that he'd always misrepresented as a safe, diplomatic attaché position. He wondered if his analogy of danger had been too close for comfort. Involvement in those situations could have cost him his life. Involvement with Summer could cost him . . . what? His peace of mind? His very soul?

The hairs on the back of his neck used to stand on end when he'd sensed that an assignment would be particularly explosive. They were standing on end at this moment. But just as he'd been unable to resist the lure of danger for fifteen years, so he seemed unable to resist it now. Derek was taking on one more assignment. He wanted Summer Reed. He intended to have her.

He'd tried to fight his attraction to her. Hadn't he?

Yes, he had. He'd lost the battle. He wanted her. She wasn't exactly the type of woman he'd thought he was looking for when he'd decided to settle down into a more normal life, but what the hell. He wasn't exactly the type of man he'd presented to the world during the past few months, either.

Oh, yes, he wanted her. Defiant, eccentric, impudent, unpredictable and vulnerable Summer. But could he make her want him? Was she so convinced that he was a dull, regimented businessman that she would refuse to acknowledge there was something exciting between them? Would she be more interested in him if he told her about what he had really done for the government?

No, dammit, he was no storybook hero, despite his past. She'd take him as he was now, or not at all.

Derek Anderson was a man of action. Quick to make decisions, quick to act on them. He went to sleep still making his plans for his campaign to win the heart and trust of Summer Reed.

"LET ME GET THIS STRAIGHT. My brother invited you over for a swim and a barbecue and you went? You spent the entire afternoon and evening with him?" Connie stared across the tiny dinette table, her green eyes wide with surprise as they focused on her roommate.

"Yep." Summer swallowed her first sip of morning coffee, her eyes closing in momentary pleasure. How she loved that first sip of coffee.

"And you had breakfast with him Saturday?"

"That's right. I'd have told you all about it last night, but you got in so late. I just couldn't wait up for you." Actually, Summer had not wanted to tell Connie everything the night before. She had needed the time to sort out her thoughts about what had happened between her and Derek yesterday. And she'd finally reached a conclusion. "Your brother is the most arrogant, high-handed, exasperating man I ever met in my life."

Connie laughed shortly. "I hear that," she muttered, using an expression she'd picked up from her Arkansan friend.

"Why didn't you tell me that he takes revenge when someone manages to get the best of him?"

"I've told you that he hates to be bested. What did you do to him, and how did he get his revenge?" Connie asked curiously.

"All I did was demonstrate how frustrating it is for someone to try to tell a person how to live his or her life," Summer explained rather obscurely, though Connie seemed to have no difficulty following the garbled explanation. "I thought I was helping you out, and you'll be glad to know that I think he finally got the message about interfering."

"If you're right, I'll owe you my eternal gratitude. But I take it you demonstrated in such a way that he felt it necessary to take revenge?"

"I'm afraid so," Summer answered glumly.

"Gulp. How'd he do it?"

"He made a heavy pass at me—several of them, actually."

Connie choked, then sputtered with laughter. "Joke, right?"

"No. Your brother assaulted me. The first time he said it was to shut me up, and after that I think he just did it because he knew I couldn't think of a thing to say in retaliation."

"He kissed you?" Connie asked in awe. "Not once but several times? And *you* were at a loss for words?"

Summer plopped her elbows on the table and cupped her cheeks in her hands. "Connie, your brother should be declared a lethal weapon. His kisses short-circuited my mental facilities. I mean, we're talking smoke out of the ears and sparks flying and hair standing on end."

"Wow!"

"You don't have to look quite so proud of him," Summer grumbled.

"It's just . . . Derek!" Connie shook her head, dazed. "Who'd a thought it?"

Summer sighed deeply. "He must have had a good laugh when he got home last night. I was a basket case by the time he dropped me off here, and he knew it."

"Maybe he was serious. Maybe he really is interested in you."

"Connie, the man said I have an idiotic life-style, that I have kooky friends and that the Salvation Army would turn up its nose at our apartment and its humble furnishings. He also said that I have no ambition and that I'm wasting my life. Does that sound like he's interested in me?"

"No," Connie admitted. "It sounds like something he'd say about me."

"Well, actually, he was talking about you, but it's the same difference."

"Thanks a lot."

"Anyway, he told me himself that I'm not his type. So why else would he have kissed me except to punish me for being right about him not having any right to interfere in your life?"

Connie kept her answer to herself, choosing, instead, to ask curiously, "He's a good kisser, huh?"

Summer turned soulful eyes at her amused roommate. "Connie, he's the best. It's a shame he's your brother so you can't find out for yourself."

"Hmm. I have to admit that he's earned himself a few points in my estimation of him. I would have thought he'd kiss as properly and conservatively as he does everything else."

"Hah!"

"What are you going to do now?"

"I'm going to forget it ever happened," Summer answered determinedly, wishing she believed her own words. "Maybe he will have forgotten it, too, by next weekend. Or at least he'll probably have decided to leave me alone. The joke's over."

"What's next weekend?"

"He's having a cocktail party for some of his clients. He wants you to serve as his hostess."

"Me?" Connie exclaimed in surprise, then shot her friend a stern look. "Whose idea was that?"

"His very own. He probably wanted to tell you about it himself, but I'm too annoyed with him to care."

"Well, he can just forget it. I'm not going to do it."

Summer blinked in surprise. Connie's reaction was something she hadn't expected. "You're not? Why?"

"Why should I?" Connie demanded belligerently, glaring down at her coffee. "Why should I do Derek any favors?"

For the first time Summer was conscious of a genuine surge of vexation at her roommate's attitude toward her brother. "Because he's going to ask you to. He's trying to make peace, Connie. Why won't you at least meet him halfway?"

"He's got you taken in, Summer. This is just another way to manipulate me. He's asking me to help out with his boring cocktail party to point out the contrast to the party you and I threw last week. He'll probably lose no opportunity to inform me that *his* is the proper type of social entertainment."

"I think you're overreacting. He's giving the party, anyway, whether you serve as his hostess or not," Summer pointed out logically. "He's trying to show you that he trusts you to help him out without embarrassing him. That he respects you, Connie."

"Why are you taking Derek's side in this?" Connie demanded. "Are you in some kind of conspiracy with him? Just what did the two of you say about me yesterday, anyway?"

"Connie!" Summer set down her coffee cup and glared at her roommate. "You know better than that."

Connie sighed. "You're right. I'm sorry. I've just gotten too used to having to search Derek's every action for ulterior purposes. You really think he's doing this as a peace offering?"

"Yes, I do," Summer answered flatly, not certain herself of why she was so sure of Derek's motives. She only knew that she trusted him and she had believed him when he'd said he wanted to be closer to his sister. And she knew that she wanted to help. "Will you do it?" she asked.

Connie grimaced. "I'll probably hate every minute of it, but I guess I will. But I warn you, we may all regret this."

"I don't think you will," Summer assured her, devoutly hoping she was right. "Anyway, he invited me to the party, as well," she said, hoping that fact would make Connie more enthusiastic about the event. Forgetting that only moments before she had urged Connie to trust Derek, she added in a mutter, "He probably hopes I'll do something to embarrass myself. Well, I'll show him that I can conduct myself as properly and respectably as . . . as Joanne Payne."

Connie looked closely at Summer's flushed face and gleaming blue eyes. "Summer, you're not actually . . . interested in my brother, are you?"

"Interested?" Summer tried very hard to sound incredulous. "Connie, does Derek seem like the hero-type to you?"

"Well, no . . ."

"I categorically refuse to give in to an attraction to a stuffy businessman. Even if he does kiss like an angel."

Again Connie remained wisely silent, though her eyes brimmed with sudden smothered laughter. "This should prove to be interesting," she murmured after a moment.

Summer glared at her and drained her coffee. "I'm going to get ready for work," she announced haughtily, rising to her full height with immense dignity.

Connie giggled and allowed herself to waste a few moments contemplating a tempestuous love affair between her sober brother and her happy-go-lucky roommate. It might definitely be interesting, she told herself gaily. Suddenly the idea of Derek's cocktail party didn't sound so bad.

"ARE YOU SURE I look all right?" Connie fretted on the doorstep of her brother's home. She smoothed the skirt of her dark green strapless cocktail dress over her well-rounded hips, then straightened the scanty bodice, which clung as if by magic to her full breasts. The auburn hair, which was usually worn in a heedless riot of curls, had been subdued into a sleek chignon at the base of her slender neck.

"Connie, you look beautiful," Summer assured her friend firmly. Summer hadn't been present when Derek had asked his sister to attend this party, so she didn't know exactly what had been said, but she assumed the conversation had been amicable enough. Connie was here. "Derek will be proud to have you as a hostess. How about me? Do I look okay?"

"More than okay," Connie replied sincerely. "You look fantastic."

Summer had chosen an interestingly draped silk jumpsuit of a rich blue that made her eyes seem more incredibly vivid than ever, reflecting the sparkle of rhinestone buckles at her shoulders and tiny waist. A cut crystal pendant glinted from the deep décolletage, and matching earrings twinkled in delicate cascades from her earlobes. A spray of white baby's breath was clipped at one side of her ultrashort hair to feminize the style for the evening, though Summer's appearance left no doubt about her gender.

Summer lifted one foot and scowled at it, eyeing the delicate straps of her silver sandals beneath the tight ankle-length hem of her jumpsuit. "If only I could wear those deadly four-inch heels like you've got on," she mourned. "There's just something dangerous about a woman in four-inch spike heels."

Connie laughed. "You would definitely be dangerous in four-inch heels, my friend. You don't walk that great in flats."

Summer's gurgle of laughter was cut short by a low growl from the door, which neither of them noticed had been opened during their mutual admiration. "That wasn't funny, Connie."

Summer rolled her eyes at her friend, adequately concealing that she was a bundle of nerves at Derek's sudden, silent appearance. Especially since he looked so damned sexy in his dark, European-cut suit. "I knew there was something we forgot, Connie," she quipped. "Cue cards."

"Cue cards?"

"Yeah. To tell Derek when to laugh. He has trouble recognizing a joke, you see."

Connie giggled. "He always has."

"Are the two of you going to stand on my doorstep and insult me all evening, or would you care to come in?" Derek inquired dryly.

Connie swept past her brother with stylish panache. "Good evening, Derek. Is everything ready?" she asked in an exaggeratedly cultured voice.

"Yes, everything's ready," he replied, watching Summer as she limped past him in Connie's wake. "Both of you look beautiful."

"Thank you, dahling," Connie returned with a regal nod of her red head. "And please take note that we are thirty minutes early, just as you dictated, er, requested."

"Connie."

"Yes, Derek?"

"Stuff it."

Connie laughed. "What did you do to Derek last weekend, Summer?" she demanded of her unusually quiet friend. "He sounds almost like a normal older brother. You must have loosened him up." She stumbled over the latter words, remembering too late how they must sound in light of what Summer had told her about the events of the previous weekend.

Summer shot eye-daggers at her roommate, but her smile was convincingly natural as she glanced at Derek, automatically noting that his eyes were gleaming almost silver. So Connie's remark had amused him, had it? Perhaps he thought that Summer would blush and stammer in confusion at the implied reminder of his devastating kisses. Well, she'd show the arrogant male that he wasn't the only one who could keep his opponent off balance. "I certainly tried my best," she murmured in answer to Connie's comment, allowing her eyes to hold Derek's for an extra moment before sliding coyly away.

"Is there anything I can do before the guests arrive, Derek?" Connie interceded hastily, though her round face was alight with suppressed laughter.

"You can make a run-through of the tables, if you like," he replied. "The caterers have everything set up, but you could just check to make sure it's all satisfactory."

"No problem." Connie walked away, admirably confident on her spike heels. She winked back at Summer just before she disappeared through the doorway into the living room.

Summer would have followed her friend, but Derek's hand on her elbow stopped her. She lifted an inquiring eyebrow at him, finding him to be making a slow, thorough examination of her from head to toe—just as he had done when she had opened her door to him early last Saturday morning. Once again she had the sensation that the examination had been more than visual. She could almost feel the warmth of his touch on her breasts, her waist, her hips. She knew the warmth was reflected in her cheeks.

"You look lovely," he said at length, lifting his eyes back to her face.

"Thank you, Derek." She would have stepped away from him, but his hand tightened on her elbow, detaining her.

"I've thought about you a great deal during the past week," he informed her, his gaze holding hers as captive as his hand held her arm.

She swallowed. "I'm sure you have," she replied coolly. Probably laughed himself to sleep every night over the way he'd shattered her composure on Sunday. "Excuse me, I'll go see if Connie needs my assistance."

"She doesn't," Derek answered bluntly. "You're not afraid to be alone with me, are you, Summer?"

Determined to keep up with him this time, she placed a beautifully manicured hand on his dark sleeve and lightly rubbed his arm through the expensive fabric. "Of course I am, Derek," she answered seductively. "You know I just don't trust myself around you."

The gleam in his eyes became more pronounced, but he didn't smile. Instead, he lowered his head to nuzzle her crystal-enhanced ear, murmuring softly, "You know what they say about playing with fire, Summer-love."

"Mmm," she replied as quietly, her heart slamming against the walls of her chest. "Sometimes you burn exactly what you intend to burn."

"Meaning me?"

"I don't know. Are you feeling warm, Derek?" she asked sweetly.

"I'm beginning to," he answered, turning his face so that his mouth grazed her cheek.

Her lids began to drift downward, then shot back up when Connie's voice interrupted from the doorway into the living room. "If you're hungry, Derek, the canapés look delicious."

"I prefer nibbling on your roommate," Derek shot back easily though he stepped away from Summer and offered her his arm. "I seem to have kept you in the foyer, Summer. Please come in."

"Why, thank you, Derek," she replied, resting her hand on his arm without a perceptible pause. Nothing about her relaxed, poised stance would indicate that her

mind was reeling and her senses vibrated wildly from
that intimate moment with him. Avoiding Connie's
quizzical look, Summer shot a glance at Derek to find
him looking back at her with a hungry expression that
made her gulp. There was definitely something different about the man tonight. Something that made her
quite nervous.

"May I get you a drink, Summer?" he offered
smoothly.

"Yes, Derek, thank you." *I hope it's a strong one*, she
thought fatalistically. *Something tells me I'm going to
need it.*

Summer wasn't sure if she was more nervous about
the way Derek was looking at her or the idea of mingling with his guests tonight. She didn't care for parties
where she didn't know many people. She infinitely
preferred the loud, cheery bashes she and Connie usually attended, where most of the guests were from their
crowd and the new ones blended in swiftly. Unless they
were like Derek Anderson, she amended, who didn't
belong at those parties in the first place.

But tonight would not be like that. Tonight would be
formal and restrained, and Summer would be the one
who did not belong. She would have to make conversation about subjects that bored her—politics, the
economy, artsy movies with subtitles—and she would
have to make explanations about her limp. It always
happened in encounters with strangers. Some well-
meaning soul would assume she'd recently injured herself and would inquire solicitously about her, and she
would have to explain that the limp was a permanent
part of her. Then she would have to see their pity as they
told her how sorry they were. God, she hated pity. At
her parties she could make jokes about her limp, laugh

off her motorcycle-riding days, and everyone would laugh with her. She had a feeling her usual flip responses would be inappropriate tonight.

She took a rather desperate gulp of the champagne that Derek had procured for her—and she didn't even like champagne. She started to ask if he had any rum punch, then decided against it.

"What's wrong, Summer?" Derek asked perceptively, watching her grimace at the taste of the expensive champagne.

"Nothing," she assured him, not quite meeting his eyes.

"You're not nervous about tonight, are you?"

"Now why would I be nervous?" she bluffed.

"Some people would be a little intimidated before a gathering of people who are all strangers."

"I don't know about Summer, but I'm scared spitless," Connie threw in, draining her own champagne. "You usually couldn't drag me to one of these affairs. Hope I don't embarrass you tonight, Derek."

"You won't," he answered assuredly. "Have I remembered to tell you how much I appreciate your doing this for me, Connie? Parties seem to go much more smoothly when there is a hostess as well as a host, don't you think? The caterers will take care of everything, for the most part. All I want you to do is mingle and keep the conversation going, and keep an eye on the caterers to make sure the trays of canapés and drinks don't get empty. Easy, right?"

"Piece of cake," Connie answered glibly. When Derek turned away, she mouthed in Summer's direction, "Help!"

Summer laughed, steeling herself for the evening ahead. She recklessly swallowed the rest of her champagne, deciding that false courage was better than no courage at all.

# 6

THE FIRST GUESTS ARRIVED soon. Derek introduced Connie and Summer as his sister and "a very close friend." Almost from the beginning Connie and Summer seemed to take on the role of co-hostesses, both of them mingling easily with Derek's guests—more easily than Summer would have imagined earlier—and keeping a close watch on the tables. Soft music played in the background, serving as no deterrent to the subdued conversations and restrained laughter. A far cry from the party that the two spirited young women had hosted the week earlier.

Though it wasn't quite as bad as Summer had feared, she still found herself getting bored when the party was only some forty minutes along. Everything was so...so predictable. Everything except Derek. He was driving her slightly crazy.

Derek practically glued himself to Summer's side from the moment the party had begun. He included her in his conversations, frequently asked her opinion about various topics of interest and had his arm around her waist as often as not. Summer was irritably aware of the assumption being made by Derek's guests. One woman even asked how long Summer and Derek had been dating and remarked that they made a lovely couple. At first, Summer had resisted his annoying little game by trying to excuse herself whenever he approached or subtly trying to slip away from that distressingly exciting arm around her waist. But since resistance only seemed to make Derek more determined to pursue her, she soon stopped trying and willed herself to relax against him. Only Derek could have known that the sweet smiles she gave him were delivered with silent promises of retribution.

"God, I'm glad you're here tonight, Summer," Connie said with a sigh when they met in the kitchen for a quiet moment an hour after the party had begun. "I'd be going crazy if it weren't for you. This is definitely not my kind of party."

"I know," Summer commiserated. "But you're doing fine, Connie. I'm sure Derek's proud of you. Anyone who didn't know you would probably think you were a real, proper lady."

Connie snickered. "Then I'd better continue to resist the urge to turn the stereo to a loud heavy-metal station or dance on Derek's expensive coffee table. Too bad Clay's not here to liven things up, isn't it?"

Grinning, Summer nodded. "Hang in there, kid. You'll get through it. By the way, I noticed that you were fast making friends with a very attractive man with gorgeous black hair and a sexy mustache. The one in the gray suit that cost more than our combined paychecks for the past two weeks."

A mischievous smile playing at the corners of her plum-glossed mouth, Connie winked at her best friend. "Nice, isn't he? His name is Joel Tanner, and he's going to be quite wealthy, thanks to my brother. He was one of Derek's first clients."

"Married? Engaged? Gay?"

"None of the above. Those were the first three questions I asked him. I think I'll go ask him some more. Ta, darling."

An hour later they met again, this time in the rest room, where they collapsed against a marble-topped vanity table as spasms of pent-up giggles erupted from them like steam from a pressure cooker.

"Summer, I can't stand it!" Connie wailed. "I swear, if this party doesn't end soon, I'm going to scream, just to see if anyone is ill-bred enough to notice. Or maybe I'll just jump Joel's bones right there in the middle of the room. I am so totally bored."

"I thought you were going to blow it for sure when you asked that fat, stuffy banker if he'd ever considered piercing his ears and then told him he had lovely lobes," Summer commented with another giggle. "Oh, the look he gave you."

"It was nothing compared to the look my brother gave me." Connie sighed. "But I just couldn't resist. Those are absolutely the god-awfullest earlobes I ever saw. Isn't it awesome the way they wiggle back and forth when he talks? I just couldn't tear my eyes away from them."

"And I thought it was Joel you couldn't tear your eyes away from."

Connie smacked her lips expressively. "The longer this ordeal goes on, the better he looks. He asked if he could take me home when this slumber party is over. You won't mind taking a cab home alone, will you, Summer?"

"Of course not. How could I deny you your fun after you've worked so hard to please your brother?"

Connie crossed her arms in front of her and lifted a delicately arched brow at her shorter friend. "Speaking of my brother, what's with him tonight? He's placed himself constantly at your side, and when he's not with you, he's watching you from across the room."

"Tell me about it," Summer replied glumly. "I'm sure everyone here has noticed."

"What do you think it means?"

"Revenge, Connie. He's still getting back at me for daring to laugh at the great, perfect Derek Anderson. He's hoping he'll make me nervous enough that I'll do something stupid."

"Are you nervous? Nobody'd ever know to look at you."

"I just hope Derek doesn't know. He'd love it. Your brother has a weird sense of humor, Connie."

"You're telling me?" Connie chuckled.

Summer sighed and checked her appearance one more time before saying, "We have to get back to the party."

Connie groaned but obediently followed her friend from the dressing room.

"Where've you been, Summer-love?" Derek asked softly from close to Summer's ear, only minutes after she'd rejoined the party. "I missed you."

Summer shot a glare over her shoulder at his smugly bland face. "It's not going to work, Derek," she told him quietly.

"What's not going to work?" His tone was interested.

"I'm not going to lose my cool with you tonight. I know you're trying to punish me for daring to attempt to teach you a lesson about your sister, but I'm on to you now and you can just forget it. It won't work."

"I have no idea what you're babbling about."

"Yes, you do!" she argued heatedly, forgetting to hold her social smile. "The way you've been hovering over me tonight and watching me and calling me, uh . . ."

"Summer-love?" he supplied helpfully.

She grimaced. "Yes. You might as well stop it now, Derek. You've had your fun."

"Excuse me, darling, one of my guests looks like he's leaving, and I'd like to have a word with him first. I'll get back to you as quickly as I can."

Before Summer could make any sort of reply, Derek brushed her mouth lightly with his and walked away, leaving her staring openmouthed and fuming at his retreating back. Damn the man, didn't he know when to call it quits? she asked herself in a near rage. Did he have any idea what he was doing to her? Her nerves were so tight that, like overwound springs, they were in danger of snapping. She was almost quivering with a mixture of anger, chagrin and raw sexual excitement. She wondered almost desperately how the evening would end. Even as she glowered at the hard, lean man in the deceptively innocuous suit as he bent attentively over a bearded older man, she was admiring the breadth of Derek's shoulders and feeling again those powerful arms around her slender waist.

Had he really called her darling?

CONNIE MANAGED to remain at the party until most of the guests had departed, at which time she located her brother and explained that she was leaving with Joel Tanner, if Derek had no objections.

Derek did not look particularly pleased, but he merely thanked his sister for doing an excellent job as his hostess and told her that he would make sure Summer got home safely.

"It's really not necessary for you to take me home, Derek," Summer assured him when Connie and Joel had departed along with the final guests. "I can call a cab. I do it all the time."

"I'm taking you home tonight, Summer, and that's final." Derek had forgotten to use the velvety tone he'd affected throughout the evening when he'd spoken to Summer, and the words came out typically arrogant.

Summer smiled, much more comfortable now that the real Derek was showing through the facade he'd assumed for her benefit. "How can I resist when you ask so sweetly, Derek?" she murmured tauntingly.

His eyes narrowed as he realized that he'd been provoked once again into the high-handed behavior that Summer so enjoyed mocking. Ignoring the caterers, who were discreetly and efficiently clearing away all signs of the party, Derek stepped closer to Summer and slipped his arms around her waist, locking his hands behind her back. "Were you and my sister laughing at me and my guests when the two of you slipped off together so often tonight?"

She'd learned that protests had no effect on his behavior, so Summer made no comment at his familiarity, though her pulse leaped exasperatingly at his touch. Again her senses were vibrating, thrumming with excitement and a primitive form of fear. Silently ordering her traitorous body to behave itself, she reminded herself sternly that she had no business wanting this man. "It was a very nice party, Derek," she answered courteously, her face suspiciously bland. "Exactly the type of party I expected you to host."

"Meaning dull," he translated, though he did not seem particularly offended.

"I didn't say that," she pointed out, concentrating on their conversation in an effort to ignore the breadth of his chest so close to her tightening breasts. There seemed to be a Ping-Pong game going on inside her own chest, which was making it difficult to breathe naturally.

"Perhaps I should have arranged for dancing," he mused, his hands beginning to stroke Summer's back almost absently.

All too aware of the lazy movements of those hands, Summer pretended to give his comment serious thought. "It might have been nice," she agreed finally.

"It's not entirely too late," Derek informed her, drawing her even closer to him. "The music is still playing, and you and I are still here."

"But I don't dance," she reminded him in a voice that was too breathless for her own comfort.

"You can dance with me," he replied imperturbably. "Put your arms around me, Summer."

"No, Derek."

"Please."

She sighed in frustration. "What is this, another way to show me up? You know I—"

A smothering kiss cut the words off neatly. "I just remembered what it takes to shut you up," Derek growled when he lifted his head. "Now put your arms around me, Summer."

She did. When Derek began to move very slowly to the easy music, she moved stiffly with him at first. Then she began to relax as she realized his feet were barely moving and his strong arms were supporting her so that she was able to dance lightly on the toes of her right foot to balance her more fully extended left leg. Before long her arms were around his neck, her cheek against his shoulder, her eyes closed as she gave herself up to the joy of dancing for the first time in five long years. Derek's hands moved lower on her back to hold her in intimate contact as his cheek nestled against her silky amber-brown hair. Neither of them noticed when the sprig of baby's breath fell to the floor.

"This is nice," he murmured after a while.

"Yes," she whispered in reply. "It is."

"You really haven't danced since your accident?"

"No."

"Why not?"

"I was afraid to try," she admitted, then opened her eyes in surprise at her own words. What was she saying? Summer Reed never confessed to such weaknesses.

"Afraid of what, Summer?"

"Oh, nothing. Forget I said it."

His arms tightened around her. "Talk to me, Summer. What were you afraid of?"

She sighed. It was hard to concentrate when she was being held so closely to his powerful body, moving slowly to the strains of romantic music. It seemed easier to just answer honestly than to try to shrug off the subject with a wisecrack as she would have done with anyone else. "I was afraid of falling or looking awkward or otherwise making a fool of myself. And I miss the kind of dancing that I used to do, the tap and jazz that I studied for so long. I didn't think that slow social dancing would compare very well."

"Do you find this dance boring?"

Brilliant blue eyes smiled up at him through thick, half-lowered lashes. "No, Derek. I'm not bored."

"Good." He pulled her even closer and dropped his cheek to hers. The first song ended and another began, and still they swayed silently in the center of the living room, the glass wall behind them reflecting their images against the diamond-studded darkness outside their softly lighted private world. When the second

song came to an end, Summer lifted her face to speak
to him, only to forget what she'd meant to say when he
took advantage of the opportunity to kiss her long and
deeply.

"Derek," she breathed when she could speak. And
then fell silent as words eluded her. Pressed as they were
from chest to knee, she was vividly aware of the arousal
that had been growing in him since that first dance, and
he had to be aware of her own physical response as her
swollen, hard-tipped breasts were flattened against
him. Blue silk and delicate lace could not conceal that
she was stimulated by his nearness, as he was by hers.
"Oh, Derek." She sighed and tightened her arms around
his neck to pull his head back down to hers. "Kiss me
again."

"Summer," he whispered against her lips just before
his mouth opened to cover hers completely. He kissed
her as if he would devour her, as if he would learn all
her secrets with only this all-consuming embrace, and
Summer opened herself to him, holding nothing back
from him.

There was no longer any pretense of dancing. Derek
kissed her, drew back only to tilt his head to a new angle and kissed her again. Summer returned kiss for kiss,
the need for oxygen a secondary consideration to her
need for Derek.

Derek's hand moved from the small of her back to
slide between them, stopping at the deeply draped
bodice of her jumpsuit. His palm moved in a slow, cir-
cular rhythm over her hardened breasts, the silk fabric
gliding sinuously beneath his hand. Summer gasped as
her body arched instinctively toward him. His head
lowered further to drop moist, hot kisses along the delicate curve of her throat.

"Oh, Derek," she moaned, her eyes tightly closed. Nothing had ever felt so right, so natural, as his arms around her, his mouth against her skin. His hardness against her softness told her how much he wanted her, and she admitted to herself that she wanted him, too.

He kissed her deeply again as her control slipped even further. Derek loosened the front of her jumpsuit just as her back touched the sofa, and she realized hazily that he had moved her to the sofa as easily as he had guided her in their dance. His breath was ragged, as was hers, clearly audible over the soft music still pouring from the hidden speakers. She could feel his breath on her skin, hot and moist, when he pressed his lips to the upper swell of one breast.

Growing impatient, she lifted herself toward him and clutched the sides of his head, needing to feel his mouth upon her. She cried out when he obliged her by taking one pointed crest between his lips.

"So beautiful. You're so beautiful," he muttered, his tongue teasing the sensitized tip he'd captured.

Summer shuddered, feeling as if there were a fire blazing between her legs. She'd never known desire so intense, need so desperate. She plucked ineffectively at his clothing, wanting to feel those sleek shoulders beneath her palms.

Their caresses escalated until they were almost out of control. With a gasp Derek tore his mouth from her heated skin. His chest heaving, he stared at her, and Summer wondered through her mist of passion when he'd removed his glasses. "I want you, Summer," she heard him mutter through the thick fog that seemed to surround her. "I've never wanted any woman this much."

"I want you, too, Derek," she whispered, knowing it wasn't necessary to tell him with words when her body had already shown him how much she wanted him.

"Ah, Summer. Sweetheart. Make love with me. Stay with me tonight."

"B-but . . ." she stammered, knowing there was some reason she should refuse. "The caterers!" she exclaimed. No, she thought dazedly. That wasn't it.

"The caterers left a long time ago, Summer-love," he told her tenderly. "There's no one here but us. Come, darling." His arm curled gently around her, lifting her from the sofa to support her at his side.

The movement seemed to bring her out of her stupor. Going stiff in Derek's arms, Summer closed her eyes and took a deep breath. This wasn't going to work, she told herself regretfully. As much as she would like to have Derek carry her into his bedroom, she just couldn't do it. It simply wasn't in her nature to make love with a man only because it felt good at the time, with no chance of a future involved. Perhaps Derek had chosen to ignore their differences for now, but Summer could not. His wanting her didn't change the fact that he considered her a flighty party-girl, that he disapproved of her.

She refused to set herself up for heartbreak again. This time the wounds might never heal.

"I'm sorry, Derek, I can't," she said finally when she felt that her voice was under control.

He stiffened in resistance to her words. "What? What do you mean, you can't?"

Pulling away from his arms, Summer took a few steps away from him, her limp seeming more pronounced than usual, and turned to face him. "Maybe I phrased that wrong. I should have said I won't," she clarified. "I told you last weekend, Derek, I'm not in the market for an affair."

Taut with frustration, Derek shoved one hand in his pocket and the other through his hair. "Dammit, Summer, you said you wanted me."

She laced her fingers tightly in front of her. "I'll admit that I'm very attracted to you, Derek. But that doesn't mean I'm going to sleep with you. I'm not."

"We're good together, Summer. Admit it."

"No. We're too different."

"I don't think that we are," Derek countered, some of the tension beginning to leave his body. He had begun to recognize the fear behind the bravado in her eyes. "We have a lot in common, Summer. Similar tastes in many things. We've never had trouble talking. I like you, and I've enjoyed spending time with you."

He liked her. Why should those words hurt? Summer lifted her chin. "But you don't approve of me."

He hesitated. "I'm not crazy about some of your attitudes about things that I think are important, but I don't disapprove of you. I'm beginning to understand you. I suspect that there's a lot more to you than you allow the world to see, and underneath your glib facade is a complex, fascinating person. Look how well you fit in with the people who attended my party tonight. You looked perfectly at ease in a social situation that is hardly the type you're accustomed to."

She found that statement rather patronizing, and her narrowed eyes told him so. Derek seemed to be deluding himself that he could mold her into the type of woman he wanted Connie to be. How dare he think that Summer needed changing? Did he have some sort of compulsion to change people? And just how the hell did he plan to repair Summer's leg so that she could be as perfect as he probably wanted her to be? Some tiny inner voice told her that she was being unfair in her anger, but only through anger could she resist the hunger she still saw in his lambent gaze.

"I really don't think we need to discuss this any further, Derek," she told him coolly. "I like you, you're a nice guy, and I hope you and Connie manage to patch up your relationship. Sorry, but I'm not interested in anything else."

By all rights he should have been angry. Instead, he was incredibly gentle when he cupped her face in his hand. "Summer, I'm not going to try to force you to make love with me if you're not ready. That's not the way I want it to be between us. But don't try to tell me you're not interested."

She trembled at his touch, wanting nothing more than to throw herself into his arms. Why was he being so damned understanding? Why wasn't he snarling at her, shouting at her, anything to help her resist him? Surely he could only be contemplating an affair. He would amuse himself with her for a while, then go off in search of a woman more like himself. And Summer would be devastated.

He'd certainly never mentioned any permanent relationship with Summer. Only that he liked her and he wanted to sleep with her. Not that she should expect anything more from him after only a week, she told herself candidly. But still, the thought of making herself so vulnerable to Derek terrified her. The intensity of her feelings for him frightened her.

She'd known so much pain.

"I'm not going to bed with you, Derek," she told him bravely. "Not tonight and not ever."

He dropped a kiss on her nose, startling her into a gasp, then stepped away from her. "Don't make promises you can't keep, Summer-love," he advised her with a note of humor in his gentle, deep voice. "Now get your purse and I'll take you home. For now." He crossed his arms over his chest in a gesture that seemed to imply the debate had ended and he considered himself the victor.

*Well, he's not,* Summer told herself, straightening her clothes as she stalked away with as much dignity as her faltering walk would allow. *It's time someone teaches that man that he can't have everything his way,* she muttered silently. *And that someone is going to be me!*

The drive across the Golden Gate Bridge and on to Summer's apartment was made in a silence that fairly sizzled with unspoken challenges and resolutions. Summer didn't invite Derek inside but told him goodnight at her door in a crisp, dismissive voice. She would have marched straight inside and closed the door in his face, but he caught her to him for a hard, searing kiss that was too brief to allow her to struggle, yet long enough to leave a lasting imprint on her senses.

"Stop doing that!" she yelled when Derek released her.

"No way," he answered imperturbably. "I'll see you tomorrow, Summer."

"No, you won't."

"Yes," he answered very softly, "I will. Sleep well, Summer-love."

"You—Ooh!" The door slammed very satisfactorily behind her when she bolted into her apartment.

"That . . . that man!" she fumed aloud. "That arrogant, presumptuous, pompous, swaggering, domineering—"

"You could only be talking about my brother," Connie commented, tying the sash of a slinky gray robe as she entered the living room from her bedroom. "In which case you left out regimented, despotic, egotistical, condescending and self-righteous. I've been through the same list of adjectives many times. You can find them in the thesaurus under Derek Anderson."

"What are you doing here?" Summer asked in surprise. "I thought you and Joel would—"

"He brought me straight home!" Connie interrupted incredulously. "He drank a cup of coffee, told me I was delightful and that he would like to see me again, asked me out for dinner Wednesday night and left with a kiss."

"How was the kiss?" Summer asked, wondering if it could even begin to compare to Derek's kisses.

"On a scale of one to ten—fourteen."

"Not bad. He seemed very nice, Connie."

"Yes, he is. I really go for him, you know? And I thought he felt the same way about me. But now I don't know."

"Connie, he asked you out. Obviously he does like you. For heaven's sake, not everyone jumps into bed after knowing each other for only a few hours."

"But . . ." Connie sank to the sagging couch, looking bewildered. "Well, all the guys I know seem to expect, well, you know."

Summer sighed and ruffled her short hair, feeling suddenly old. "I keep telling you that men care about more than sex from a woman. Not many of them, it's true, but there are a few men left who function with their brains instead of their jockstraps. Your brother is not among them, I might add," she finished darkly.

"Don't tell me Derek made another pass at you."

"Did he ever. Damn the man, Connie."

"Oh, wow." Connie shook her head, her green eyes dazed. "I can't believe this is my brother we're talking about. The man is so proper and straitlaced where I'm concerned that I've thought he should be a candidate for the priesthood. Now he's trying to seduce my roomie. Did you tell him to take a hike into the Pacific?"

"He seems to have a hearing problem," Summer answered dolefully, thinking of his patient refusal to accept her attempted rejection of him. She dropped her face into her hands. "Connie, the man is driving me crazy. What am I going to do with him?"

"Honey, I've been asking myself the same question for years. He was always kind of bossy, even when he was a teenager, but ever since he went off to Vietnam and then into that mysterious government work of his, he's been like a stranger to me. That didn't keep him from trying to run my life long-distance," she added bitterly. "God, I get so tired of trying to live up to his expectations."

Which was exactly the reason Summer was afraid to get involved with Derek. Like Connie, she was afraid she wouldn't live up to his expectations. She could see firsthand how much it hurt to love him and not be able to please him. Still, she wished that Connie and Derek could find a way to live in some sort of harmony. After all, they were family. Reaching out a tentative hand to touch Connie's shoulder, she said carefully, "Derek does love you, Con. Very much. I've seen it in his face, and I've seen how much it hurts him when the two of you fight. I don't know why he is such a perfectionist about the people he cares for, but he must have his reasons. Maybe it's a lingering result of his experience in Vietnam. It must have been horrible."

"I know. But he won't talk about it. Ever. In fact, he rarely talks about himself. Just hands out suggestions."

Summer thought about Connie's words for a moment, realizing they were true. Derek had asked a lot of questions about her past, but he had never volunteered any information about himself.

"It's like he came home with a neat list of things to do," Connie continued glumly. "Buy a house, establish a management consulting business, reform Connie."

"If it makes you feel any better, I think I've replaced you as his next project," Summer said on a sigh.

Connie thoughtfully twirled a long red curl around one fingertip. "I noticed something different about Derek at the party tonight, Summer. With you, he's different. He teased you and smiled at you, and I could have almost sworn that the Derek I knew years ago was back. He was even more relaxed with me when you were around. I think you're good for him."

Summer shook her head quickly, not wanting to hear anything that might lead to false hopes. "No, Connie, it wouldn't work. He'd start trying to change me, and I'd hate being told what to do.

"You have a point there." Connie released the curl she'd twisted into a corkscrew tangle and stared down glumly at her crimson-painted toenails. "I don't know if it's possible for him to learn when to butt out."

For a time the two young women sat in almost identical poses, faces cradled in hands, elbows propped on knees, as they contemplated the exasperating man whom both were drawn to despite their annoyance with him. Summer was the first to rouse from their mutual stupor.

"The hell with it," she announced, pushing herself off the couch. "I'm going to bed, and I suggest you do the same thing. We'll both get a good night's sleep, and tomorrow we'll wake up fresh and ready to take on one Derek Anderson."

"You're right," Connie agreed decisively, rising to stand beside her friend. "Uh, Summer?"

"Yes, Connie?" Summer paused on the way to her bedroom to look back over her shoulder.

"What I would really like is for Derek to just love me, without qualifications, exactly the way I am. I don't suppose you'd want the same thing from him, would you?"

Summer tossed her head. "Don't be ridiculous. I'm holding out for a hero, remember? Not a stuffed-shirt businessman." She wished she could have had just a little more conviction in her voice.

"So you've gotten immune to his kisses, huh? They didn't turn you on tonight?"

Summer sighed deeply. "No more than a current of electricity turns on a light bulb. Damn the man." She closed the door firmly on Connie's sudden laughter.

# 7

IF ONLY SHE COULD close the door as resolutely on her thoughts as she had on her roommate, Summer thought much later, tossing and turning in her bed. Derek had shaken her badly tonight, especially when he'd made her realize how much she wanted to make love with him. And he'd wanted her. Why? Why would he want a woman of whom he disapproved so strongly? What was it about her that attracted him?

Even more to the point, what was it about him that attracted her? After all, he wasn't handsome. Sexy, yes. Virilely attractive, yes. Nicely built, yes. But not handsome.

And he didn't have a great sense of humor. Well, maybe he did, judging from the way he'd teased her and the suspiciously smile-like gleam that flitted so often in his lovely pewtery eyes. But he certainly did his best to keep his sense of humor hidden.

He was arrogant and overbearing. She tried to forget the gentleness he'd shown her, first when he thought he'd hurt her last Saturday and even tonight, when he should have been angry at being so abruptly rejected. How could he have been so understanding?

He was too conventional. Yes, there was one accusation that would stick. Summer craved adventure, excitement. That was why she drifted from job to job, trying to find something to replace the thrill of dancing and acting, why she hated schedules and routines, why she'd moved to an eccentric town like San Francisco, a place as different from Rose Bud, Arkansas, as anyone could possibly imagine. Derek had put excitement and adventure behind him, choosing a quiet, settled life as a businessman over his former government career. Now his idea of adventure probably consisted of trying out a new restaurant or a new brand of toothpaste.

So what did Derek see in her? Was she his thrill of the month? Did he get some kind of kick out of the idea of taking a free-spirited, lame butterfly to his bed?

Deciding that she would never decipher Derek's motives tonight, Summer rolled over in the bed, slammed her fist into her pillow a couple of times and pulled the covers to her ears. She lay still for a long moment, deliberately concentrating on clearing her mind of all thought.

Which left it open to sensation.

Once again she could feel Derek's arms around her as soft music swirled around them, could feel his lips on hers, his hands on her back, his breath and tongue on her breasts. "Dammit!" she muttered, kicking off her covers and throwing her pillow to the floor in an unwonted temper tantrum. "Get out of my bedroom, Derek Anderson!"

She plopped onto her stomach, leaving her pillow where it had fallen, and willed herself into a restless sleep.

Across the bay Derek lay in his bed and stared up at the ceiling of his bedroom, his arms behind his head. The pieces of the puzzle that made up Summer Reed were slowly beginning to come together for him. Despite her pretense of carefree sophistication, Summer was basically a sweet, somewhat old-fashioned young woman who still believed in the values she'd been taught during her childhood in Rose Bud, Arkansas. She loved to laugh but behind the laughter were tears that she would allow no one to see. Tears of disappointment for the career she'd never had a chance to pursue, tears of frustration for the unfulfilling life she'd drifted into, tears of chagrin for the uncomfortable disability that prevented her from participating in many of the activities a healthy young woman of her age enjoyed. Dancing, sports, runs on the beach. Perhaps even limited her daily activities. Shopping, walking. He'd noticed the way her limp grew even more pronounced when she'd been standing for a long time.

He hated the thought of Summer in pain. Just the idea of her lying bloody and torn on a street after the accident made him break out in a cold sweat. Did the leg still give her pain? Of course it did. He'd seen injuries like that before, in Vietnam, and they never completely healed. But she'd never let on if she *were* in pain. She'd just make a joke about it and change the subject.

She was so very vulnerable. So afraid of being hurt again. Had she really thought he didn't know that? Did she really think he'd ever do anything to hurt her? He wasn't going to let her insecurities stand between them when something much stronger was pulling them together.

Derek was beginning to suspect exactly what it was he felt for Summer Reed, though he would wait until he was sure before applying a label to his feelings. Unlike Summer, the idea of a relationship, a permanent relationship, did not frighten him at all. She was wonderful; she was everything he'd been looking for. He wanted nothing more than to make her happy.

Derek went to sleep feeling very optimistic about his future, exhilarated by his new mission.

DEREK STOOD outside Summer and Connie's apartment at nine o'clock on Sunday morning, just in case Summer had planned to leave early to avoid seeing him. He pressed the doorbell. He knew his pursuit of Summer Reed would not be an easy one. She was going to resist him. She'd spent too many years hiding her feelings to open up to him immediately. But what the heck—he'd taken on assignments with slimmer odds and won. He had every confidence he would win this time. He pressed the bell again.

It was his sister who finally opened the door, wrapped in a gray robe and nothing else, her eyes sleepy.

"Don't you think you should ask who's ringing the bell before you open the door dressed like that?" he growled in concern.

"Give me a break, Derek, I saw you through the peephole," Connie returned crossly. "Besides, rapists don't ring doorbells. They climb through windows."

"Connie, that's ridiculous." He brushed past her. "Summer still in bed?"

"Yes, she is. And she'll probably stay there until you leave." Connie ran a hand through her tangled curls and yawned. "Why don't you leave the poor girl alone, Derek? Stick to your campaign to reform me. I *have* to put up with you. You're my brother."

"Let's you and I make a deal, Con," Derek suggested casually. "You keep out of my affair with Summer, and I'll stop giving you unwanted advice."

Connie smiled brightly. "Hallelujah. Too bad you haven't a prayer of having an affair with Summer, or I'd take you up on that very tempting offer."

"I didn't mean it quite that way, but don't write me off yet. You never know what will happen." He walked past her, moving in the direction of Summer's closed bedroom door.

Connie frowned. "Derek . . ."

He glanced back without pausing. "Butt out, Connie."

For the first time Connie noticed the way her brother was dressed, and her eyes widened. A brown leather bomber jacket, white knit pullover shirt, well-worn jeans and scuffed brown biker's boots. Derek had come dressed for trouble.

Derek closed Summer's door behind him and stood looking down at her for a long moment before approaching the bed. The doorbell hadn't awakened her. She lay on her stomach, her head cradled on one arm, the other arm dangling off the side of the bed. The covers were tangled at her feet, and her legs were sprawled as carelessly as a child's, the knit nightshirt she wore hiked up to reveal green-and-white-striped panties over a shapely tush. Derek fought down the impulse to jump on top of her and walked to the head of the bed, kicking aside the pillow on the floor. He knelt beside her, pushing a large stuffed bear out of the way, and examined the sleep-flushed face beneath the short, tousled golden-brown hair. The faintest purple rings under her long, closed lashes indicated that she hadn't slept well. Had her rest been disturbed by thoughts of him?

God, she was lovely. His insides twisted with a desire so powerful that it rocked him back on his heels. He'd never wanted a woman this much in his life.

Very slowly he leaned forward until his lips just brushed a down-soft cheek. She tasted good. So very good. He touched his lips in a butterfly caress to the end of her adorably tilted nose. Her velvety eyelid received a fleeting salute before his roving mouth touched the

corner of her slightly parted lips. Her breath was warm
and soft against his skin, and he kissed her mouth
again. She stirred, and the beginnings of a smile
touched her face. "Derek," she murmured without
opening her eyes.

A wave of emotion surged through him, so intense
that he nearly doubled over from the force of it. "Yes,
Summer, it's Derek," he whispered, his voice hoarse.

Her smile deepened, her eyelashes fluttering on her
cheeks. Blinking at the light, she squinted shyly up at
him. "Hi, Derek," she murmured, sleep still deepening
her voice.

"Oh, God, Summer." Unable to resist any longer,
Derek leaned over the bed and took her in his arms, his
mouth covering hers in a kiss that was as hungry as it
was gentle. She made a sound like a purr deep in her
throat and lifted her arms to slide them around his neck,
her lips opening to his without hesitation. Derek knew
she was still half-asleep but took full advantage of her
momentary weakness as he lowered himself beside her
and deepened the kiss.

Stretching like the cat whose purr she imitated,
Summer snuggled into Derek's embrace, luxuriating in
his warmth and strength. His mouth moved against
hers, his tongue stroking hers in a kiss that was even
more beautiful than those that had haunted her dreams.
Holding herself even closer to him, she silently begged
for his touch. As if she'd moaned the request aloud, he
gave her what she desired, his hand sliding across her
back and around her waist to cup her breast. Summer
whimpered and held him more tightly, arching into his
palm. Derek lifted his head only to pull in a shudder-
ing breath, then kissed her again. His hand moved fe-
verishly over her scantily clad figure, discovering and

stroking all her feminine secrets. Summer felt as if she were on fire. She wanted him. Oh, how she wanted him.

And then his hand moved over her hip and down her thigh, slipping behind her knee to lift her leg over his. Her right knee. She flinched as the mangled joint, always stiff in the morning, protested the movement with a twinge of pain.

Dismayed, she tore her mouth away from Derek's and pushed against his chest, fully awake. "What the hell are you doing in my bedroom?" she said on a gasp, scooting back on the bed to put a safe distance between them.

Reluctantly acknowledging that the golden moment was over, Derek made no effort to detain her but lifted himself slowly onto his elbow, looking at her with a rueful smile. "I would think the answer to that question is obvious," he told her huskily.

"You came here to seduce me?" she demanded, crossing her arms defensively over her chest. "In my own bedroom?"

Something about the outraged question struck him as funny, and he chuckled. Then, as her eyes narrowed in sudden fury, he realized that laughter was not exactly the most tactful response to this particular situation. "I only came in here to wake you," he assured her gravely, pushing himself upright to stand beside the bed, easing his hands into the pockets of his painfully tight jeans as he did so. "I'll admit that things got a little out of control, but I'm certainly not apologizing. I thought it was fantastic. You were enjoying it, too. Admit it."

"I was asleep!" she protested, pushing her bangs out of her eyes with a trembling hand.

"You knew what you were doing," he answered relentlessly. "You called me by name."

Flushing vividly, she dropped her eyes from his, frowning as she took in his casual attire. "Your clothes."

"What about them?"

"They make you look . . . different."

"You asked me if I own a pair of jeans. You see now that I do."

Thoroughly disoriented, Summer shook her head as if clearing the last vestiges of sleep, then glared at him. "What are you doing in my bedroom?" she asked again.

He just couldn't help it. He chuckled again. "We've already been through that, remember? You look wonderful in the mornings. Even if your hair *does* tend to stand straight up." His eyes made a lazy survey of the skimpy nightshirt that had proved so little barrier against his wandering hands. The words printed across the front of the orange knit shirt darkened his eyes: Motorcycle Mama. "That shirt is sick."

"Connie gave it to me. I think it's cute."

"You would. Get dressed. We're spending the day together."

"The hell we are."

He sighed. "Look, Summer, you can either get dressed and go out with me, or we'll spend the entire day right here in your bed. Personally, I'd prefer the latter, but something tells me that you wouldn't agree."

"You're damned right I don't agree."

"Then get dressed. I'll go find some coffee and wait for you."

"Derek, you can't just walk into my bedroom and tell me that I'm going to spend the day with you."

"I just did. See you in half an hour." He winked at her as he walked toward the door.

Summer groped for her pillow, hoping to find it in time to throw it at his retreating back. Too late she remembered that she'd thrown it to the floor the night before. With one last insolent glance back at her Derek walked out of the room, quietly closing the door behind him.

Her head buzzing with conflicting emotions, Summer took her shower. A cold shower. Even that could not quench the fires Derek had started within her. Damn him! She'd never met anyone like him. Though she'd met some single-minded, intractable, persistent males in her life, Derek should win a prize. When he set his mind on something, he intended to achieve it regardless of the consequences. Not through flashy, ostentatious, creative measures, but by steady, thorough, relentless pursuit. No grand hero, this Derek Anderson, but a man who achieved his goals quietly. Not qualities she normally admired in a man. So why did she find them so utterly fascinating in Derek? And why was she beginning to resign herself to the fact that an affair with him was fast becoming inevitable?

While she dressed in an oversize white fleece top and baggy stone-washed jeans, her rational side continued to remind her of the reasons she must resist the temptation to give in to Derek, even as her body throbbed with the remnants of passion he'd created upon awakening her. She told herself that she had taken an unusual amount of time with her makeup only to hide the aftereffects of her restless night, not to look particularly attractive for Derek. Sliding her feet into the stylish leather flats that she wore from necessity as well as fashion, she took a deep breath before heading for the door through which Derek had departed only twenty minutes earlier.

She found him in the kitchen, sharing coffee with his sister. Summer wasn't particularly surprised to discover that they were talking about Joel.

"Did you know him before he hired you to look over his business?" Connie was asking as Summer entered the room. "Joel was a little vague about how the two of you met."

"I've known him for a while," Derek answered.

"Oh, great. You're about as helpful as he was," Connie complained. "Don't you like him, Derek?"

Derek looked steadily at her. "Now how should I answer that? If I tell you that I don't like him and wish you wouldn't see him, you'll throw yourself into his arms. If I encourage you to see him because he's a decent guy and would be good for you, you'll drop him like a hot rock."

Summer swallowed a chuckle at Derek's wickedly accurate assessment. He obviously had no intention of commenting on Joel Tanner.

"Well, you should be pleased to know that your friend brought me straight home last night and told me good-night without even making a pass."

"That must have been quite a change for you," her brother muttered into his coffee.

Connie started to bristle, but Summer interceded hastily. "Good morning, Connie. Sleep well?" she asked, ignoring Derek as she limped across the room to pull a coffee mug from the cabinet.

"Until I was so rudely awakened, yes," Connie replied. "The sugar's in the sugar bowl, Summer."

"What a unique place for it. Usually we just dip it from the sack."

"Don't look at me. Derek's the one who filled the bowl."

"I should have known."

"Stop talking about me like I'm not in the room,"
Derek commanded them both, rising to his feet. "Here,
Summer, take my chair. I'll lean against the counter.
Why the hell don't you invest in some decent furniture? Surely between the two of you, you could afford
some good used furniture that isn't in danger of falling
apart."

"This furniture came with the apartment. Besides, we
have other ways we'd rather spend our money," Connie answered with a shrug. "It's not like either of us
makes that much."

Derek sighed but resisted further comment on that
particular subject. "Aren't either of you going to have
breakfast?"

Again it was Connie who answered. She lifted her
coffee cup. "You're looking at it, brother dear. How did
you think we eat as much as we do on special occa-
sions and still maintain our girlish figures?"

"But breakfast is—"

"The most important meal of the day. Honestly,
Derek, you sound like someone's grandmother."

He only grunted.

"Isn't it amazing how much meaning he can put into
that one short sound?" Connie asked Summer, smiling
across the table in a conspiratorial manner.

"You're talking about me again," Derek complained.

"It's not the first time," his sister retorted.

"I'll bet," he responded resignedly. "I'd ask you to join
Summer and me today, Connie, but I know you and
Mother are planning to visit Barbara's newest grand-
child."

"I'm only going because Mother insisted," Connie grumbled. "I dread spending even five minutes in the same room with Saint Barbara."

"Connie—"

Again Summer jumped in before the Anderson siblings came to verbal blows. "I told you earlier, Derek. I'm not spending the day with you."

"Yes, you are."

"No, I'm not. I have plans for today, and I have no intention of changing them."

He scowled. "You have a date?"

She considered using that excuse, but she wouldn't lie to him. "Well, no, not exactly a date."

His expression cleared. Rubbing his chin consideringly, he shrugged away her argument as unimportant. "Okay, I'll go with you. Where are we going?"

"You weren't invited!"

"I am now. Where are we going?"

Connie laughed. "You might as well give up, Summer. If you don't take him along, he'll just follow you."

Derek nodded genially. "That's right. Where are we going, Summer-love?"

Summer looked down at her coffee cup, her fingers twitching on the chipped handle.

Reading either her mind or her expression—Summer devoutly hoped it was the latter—Derek said softly, "I wouldn't recommend it, Summer."

Connie giggled, but Summer only glared at him. "I wouldn't dream of wasting my first cup of coffee of the day on your shirtfront," she told him loftily.

"Smart move." His mouth tilted into the grin that was making an appearance with increasing regularity, the one that made Summer want to throw herself on him and taste it.

Dismayed and even a little frightened by the strange impulses Derek aroused in her, Summer decided to go along with him without further argument. She'd let him tag along today, she determined abruptly. Later he'd be sorry he insisted. Maybe today he'd get the picture that there could be no question of a relationship between them, regardless of how brief. "I don't think I'll tell you where we're going," she told him slowly. "You're sure you don't want to back out now?"

"I'm sure." He tilted his cup, drained the contents and set the cup in the sink. "When do we start?"

"Whenever you're ready."

"I'm ready now."

She pushed herself away from the table. "Then let's go. See you later, Connie."

"Bye." Connie seemed to be holding in gales of laughter as she eyed the other two, her dancing eyes giving away the emotion she was trying to suppress. "Have fun, kids."

"Yeah," Summer muttered heavily. "You bet."

Derek assisted Summer into the passenger seat of his plush gray Lincoln—as if she needed help to climb into a car, she thought resentfully. She watched through her lashes as he slid behind the wheel. "Where to?" he asked pleasantly.

She named the nearest shopping mall.

"We're going shopping?" he asked without evidence of distaste.

"I have to buy a birthday present for Autumn," she explained. "Her birthday's next week, and I need to get the gift in the mail by tomorrow or it will never get to her on time."

He nodded. "Is that all you have planned for to-day?"

"No," she answered rather curtly. "I'll tell you the rest later."

"Fine." Still he didn't start the car but sat twisted in the seat, facing her as if he were waiting for something.

"Forget how to start it?" she inquired facetiously.

"Nope. But I'd really like to kiss you again before we leave. With you awake this time."

She flushed. "Forget it," she told him gruffly.

He kept his face suspiciously innocent though the corners of his mouth twitched. "Not even a little one?" he asked hopefully.

She sighed. "What is it with you and kissing, Derek? Don't you ever think of anything else?"

She knew she'd asked the wrong question as soon as the words were out of her mouth. Derek laughed. A quick, unexpected laugh that seemed to startle him almost as much as it did her. "Yes, Summer, I think of something else. I could elaborate in great detail, if you'd like."

"No, that's not necessary," she told him hastily, cheeks burning, though her heart was fluttering crazily in response to his wonderful laugh. He'd actually laughed, she told herself wonderingly, and her own lips curved into an answering smile.

"Well?" he asked humorously. "May I kiss you? Or are you only brave in your sleep?"

He shouldn't have made it sound like a challenge. Summer never could resist a challenge. "I'm not afraid to kiss you, Derek," she told him flatly. "I can control my emotions."

"Prove it."

She reached out a hand and grabbed him by the shirt collar, tugging to bring him closer. She leaned forward in her seat to meet him halfway, stopping just short of completing the embrace. When he moved no further, she swallowed. It was clearly up to her to do the kissing this time, she realized nervously. Derek was calling her bluff. Hesitating only a fraction of an inch from his firm mouth, she inhaled, then pressed her lips to his.

Surely she'd only meant to give him a brief, friendly kiss, she told herself dazedly a long time later. It surely couldn't have been her intention to extend the caress into a passionate clinch that had threatened to steam the windows of the car and melt all the plastic on the instrument panel.

It wasn't even Summer who pulled away first. Derek was breathing raggedly when he pulled back and sat her firmly in her seat, running his hand through his hair as he turned back to the steering wheel. "I think we'd better go to the mall," he said huskily, "before I think of a good use for that nice big back seat."

Summer clenched her hands in her lap and stared down at them, grateful for small favors. At least he hadn't teased her for allowing the kiss to get so wildly out of control.

If Summer had expected Derek to be disconcerted when she walked straight into a small boutique that specialized in expensive lingerie, she was destined to be disappointed. He strolled into the shop with the ease of a man who'd spent many pleasant hours in such places. Perhaps he had, Summer thought glumly. He stood quietly aside as Summer selected a luscious black nightgown for her fiery-spirited, auburn-haired sister.

"This is for the liberated sister?" he inquired with a lifted brow, examining the filmy scrap of froth.

"Yep," Summer replied cheerfully, picturing Autumn's exasperation upon opening the gift. "I like to remind her occasionally that she *is* a woman."

"Maybe you should try it on so we can get an idea of how it would look on," Derek suggested with an exaggerated leer.

Summer firmly declined, though she had to turn her face to hide the flush that accompanied several unbidden fantasies of herself wearing such a garment for Derek.

While she was in the mall, Summer made several other purchases, items she'd waited until the weekend to stock up on. She blithely loaded Derek down with her packages.

"Is there anything else you'd like to buy before we leave the mall?" he asked her politely, his arms full. "Like a couple of dozen pairs of shoes?"

"No, thanks," Summer replied airily. "Come along, Derek."

Her charming attempt at imperiousness delighted him so much that he stopped right in the middle of the crowded mall to kiss her, earning himself a glare and another one of her rosy blushes.

"I'm hungry," she told him when they were back in the car. "Why don't we have some lunch somewhere?"

He agreed very cooperatively and took her to Fisherman's Wharf, spending the quiet time during the meal learning more about her childhood years in Arkansas. She answered his questions stiffly at first, but Derek's genuine interest in her words put her quickly at ease. Soon she was chattering away, making him smile and once even laugh with her stories of her boisterous childhood.

Summer even managed to draw Derek out enough to talk a bit about his own childhood. He admitted that he had been quite a handful, always tumbling into trouble and making frequent visits to the emergency room.

"When did you turn into such a respectable citizen?" Summer asked him with gentle mockery.

He grimaced at her but answered semiseriously. "Probably about the time Connie was born. My father told me that I had to set a proper example for my baby sister, since I was so much older."

"How did you feel about having a little sister after being an only child for so long?" Summer asked curiously.

Derek lifted one shoulder, his expression almost wistful. "I thought it was nice. She was cute, as babies go, and I used to enjoy playing with her. But then I ended up in Nam and drifted into the government job, and before I knew it, she was grown-up and practically a stranger. I don't know what happened, exactly."

Her heart twisting at the sadness in his eyes, Summer reached across the table to touch his hand. "You made a good start at repairing the damage last night, Derek. The two of you were a little more relaxed together this morning."

"Yeah, I think so, too," he answered, looking faintly pleased.

Summer released his hand, aware of her reluctance to do so. "How do you really feel about Connie dating Joel?" she asked Derek, forcing herself to keep her mind on their conversation.

To Summer's surprise Derek broke into a broad grin. "I find it very amusing," he informed her cryptically.

Summer frowned in confusion. "Why?"

But Derek only shook his head. "I'll tell you another time," he told her, refusing to say another word about it.

When the meal was over, Derek asked again, "Where to?"

She gave him a rueful smile. "I hope you're feeling rested and refreshed. Our next stop is Halloran House."

He frowned. "Halloran House?"

"It's a home for children with emotional or behavioral problems. It's Clay McEntire's pet project—he spent some time in a similar home when he was growing up, and he doesn't mind telling people that he would have ended up in prison by now if he hadn't received excellent counseling and guidance at the youth home. Anyway, the kids at Halloran House are putting on a talent show. Clay volunteered my services to them when he found out that I'd been a theater arts major. They've been rehearsing on Wednesday evenings and Saturday mornings, but they're putting on the show this coming Friday and they wanted to work in one extra rehearsal today. You can just drop me off if you don't want to stay."

"I'll stay." The words were spoken decisively. Derek was vaguely aware that he was enjoying himself more than he could have imagined. The more time he spent with Summer Reed, the more she fascinated him. And the more he wanted her. "What's the address?"

# 8

HALLORAN HOUSE HAD been established in a large, renovated Victorian home by a wealthy industrialist who had lost a son to a drug overdose, Summer explained as Derek drove. It relied on donations for its continued existence, many of which were obtained from wealthy families whose children had been in trouble with drugs or other serious adolescent problems. Though most of the children in residence at Halloran House were from low-income families, there were some there from the middle and upper classes. Mostly between the ages of eleven and sixteen, these were kids who, either because of neglect at home or the influence of their peers, had gotten beyond the control of their parents and teachers, though they had not yet been convicted of any real crimes.

Summer was greeted warmly by the Halloran House residents, though Derek was not welcomed with open arms. The troubled young people there did not trust adult strangers, and they looked him over thoroughly when Summer introduced him. Derek was grateful that he'd chosen to dress in leather jacket and jeans that morning. His short, almost military haircut earned him enough suspicious looks. His usual crisp white shirts and dark, creased slacks would have put him in contempt with these defiantly ragged youths with their too old eyes.

In the cavernous, one-time ballroom, which now
served as a recreation room, a stage had been erected
and a stereo, with huge blaring speakers, set up. Young
people were practicing all over the room, oblivious to
the chaos around them. At least half a dozen different
pop songs were being mangled simultaneously, danc-
ers were leaping like demented deer, a teenage girl
dressed like Cyndi Lauper was swaying sinuously, another was twirling a baton and a group in one corner
seemed to be loudly practicing a comedy skit. Summer
had told Derek that there were only twenty full-time
residents. Ten more attended counseling sessions there
after school while living at home. Not all of those
would be involved in the show, but to Derek there
seemed to be hundreds of noisy adolescents in the
room.

Through the confusion they heard a male voice yell
"Summer!" and the rugged blond that Derek remembered from Connie and Summer's party broke away
from the crowd and came quickly across the room. He
greeted Summer with an enthusiastic kiss on the mouth,
which brought a murderous scowl to Derek's tanned
face.

"Derek, do you remember Clay McEntire?" Summer asked. "Clay, this is Connie's brother, Derek. He
was at our party last weekend."

The two men shook hands—Derek with some reluctance—but before they could do more than murmur
appropriate greetings, another man approached. A
prematurely balding fellow of about thirty with thick
glasses and a seemingly permanent grin, he was introduced by Summer as Frank Rivers, the director of Halloran House. " 'Bout time you got here, Summer. We've
got a madhouse on our hands."

"No problem," Summer assured him airily, then cupped her hands and shouted, "All right, you animals, the director's here. Let's show a little respect."

Magically the chaos subsided. Laughing, the kids gathered around Summer, who ordered them to sit on the floor in front of the stage. Derek was rather astonished when they obeyed her without question. Summer dispatched him to a straight-backed chair in one corner of the room to watch the proceedings. Like the kids, he did as she told him without protest.

For the next two hours Derek watched in fascination as Summer turned the eighteen insolent delinquents attending the rehearsal into surprisingly adequate performers. Laughing, teasing and cheerfully insulting, she had the kids eating out of her hand, even as she managed to maintain control of the rehearsal with very little help from Frank and Clay. She applauded each performance, offered suggestions when needed, even walked through the Cyndi Lauper routine with the girl, smoothing out the rough edges of the lip-synched pantomime. Despite the enforced awkwardness of her movements, Summer maintained a graceful fluidity that Derek knew had been developed through long grueling hours of therapy and practice. The talent that had won her the role of Eliza Doolittle was very much in evidence.

Later he was given a sample of her singing talent when a shy, pretty teen with chocolaty eyes and a smooth mocha complexion requested assistance with a song she planned to sing, particularly with one measure that was giving her problems. Summer glanced at the music, murmured a few words to the woman who had been recruited to play the piano and sang the song in a key that was much easier for the young person to carry.

As the rehearsal concluded, Summer again walked through the closing number with the entire cast, a simply choreographed version of the title song from the movie *Fame*. Derek frowned as he noticed that Summer's limp was growing more and more pronounced. Searching her face, he thought she looked tired. He was considering dragging her off the stage and making her take a rest when she called an end to the rehearsal.

Summer sincerely complimented the performers as they left her, promising to see them Wednesday night for their final rehearsal before the show on Friday evening. As she said her goodbyes and made her last-minute remarks, Clay approached Derek. "She's good, isn't she?"

"Yeah," Derek answered simply. "She's good."

"I knew this would be good for her, but I had a hell of a time talking her into it."

"Oh?" Derek studied the pleasure on Summer's tired face as she looked into the young faces turned to her. "I'd have thought she'd jump at the chance to do something like this."

"I think she was afraid she couldn't do it," Clay explained in a low voice. "You might not have realized it, but our Summer's not quite as carefree as she lets on. We all know that she's a little sensitive about her limp, but she's brave about it, isn't she?"

Resenting Clay's thinking he might know more about Summer—Derek's Summer, not *our* Summer, he added to himself—Derek only nodded. He was a little deflated to realize that he wasn't the only one who understood the complex young woman who had come to mean so much to him in such a short time. He was also jealous as hell of anyone who had known her longer than he had. He glared at Clay as Summer approached them.

"Sorry it took so long, Derek. Are you bored out of your mind?"

He slipped a supportive and unmistakably possessive arm around her waist. "Not a bit," he assured her, his voice husky and intimate. "Tired, Summer-love?"

"Mmm. A little," she agreed, not protesting the supportive arm.

"Then let's go." He gave her little chance to say goodbye to Frank or the avidly curious Clay as he hustled her out the door and into his car.

Summer sank gratefully into the plush seat of the Lincoln, resting her head against the high back. "Weren't they wonderful?" she asked Derek huskily.

"I felt like I was watching one of those old Mickey Rooney and Judy Garland movies," he confessed. "The ones where they're always saying 'Let's have a show!'"

Summer laughed softly. "Kids haven't changed all that much over the years. They still love attention, and they need to know they have special talents that make them worthy of praise. Even the ones who can't sing or dance were able to participate in the skits or operate the lights or sound system, so they feel like an important part of the show. Basically, these kids are the ones who crave attention so desperately that they got into trouble to impress their friends or get their parents to notice them."

Out of the corner of his eye Derek watched as Summer kneaded her right leg almost absently. He frowned. But rather than commenting on her action, he asked only, "Who will attend the show?"

"The parents and some of the home's benefactors. Not that many people—there's not an abundance of room." Pulling her thoughts away from the rehearsal, she turned her attention to the route Derek was taking. "Where are you going?"

"My place."

She turned to look at him. "I never said I was finished for the day. I might have other plans."

"Tough," he answered succinctly. "You need to rest. We're going to my place, and I'm going to make dinner for you."

Summer considered her options. She could berate him for his arrogance and order him to take her home, or she could go along with his autocratic and typically domineering decree. Judging from the hard set of his jaw, she had little chance of success with the first option. He'd do what he wanted to do, anyway.

A little smile played on her tired features as she settled back more comfortably into the seat, realizing that she wanted the same thing.

SUMMER STRETCHED and opened her eyes, then gasped as she looked frantically at her watch. Sitting up on the bed in Derek's guest room, she realized that she'd been asleep for just over an hour. She had protested heatedly when he'd ordered her to lie down and rest as soon as they were in the house, but he'd stubbornly insisted that she would either lie down alone or he would join her.

She had hastily agreed to lie down alone.

She hadn't expected to be able to relax, much less sleep. A near sleepless night followed by an unusually strenuous day had caught up with her, however. Now she was a little embarrassed.

She wondered what Derek had done during the time she'd been asleep. Had he looked in on her? She didn't like the idea of being so vulnerable to his knowing eyes twice in one day.

Combing her hair with her fingers, she thought back over the past few hours. It had been wonderful having Derek by her side all day, she mused wistfully. She could easily get used to having him around all the time. She thought of his willingness to stay on the sidelines during the rehearsal, his cheerful acquiescence at the mall, his stubborn protectiveness when he'd seen that she was tired.

Oh, yes, she sighed, pushing her feet into her Loafers, she could definitely grow accustomed to his company. She'd known him only a little more than a week, and already she was dreading the idea of a weekend without him. For a woman who'd placed so much value on her independence in the past few years, the realization of how easily she could become emotionally dependent on Derek was quite daunting.

She hadn't relied on anyone but herself for her happiness in a long time. Now she was starting to shift toward Derek. She didn't care for that one bit. But it was too late to do anything about it now except to hang on fiercely to whatever willpower she had left. Which wasn't much.

Sighing, she straightened her clothes and went in search of Derek.

She found him reading a newspaper in the den. He didn't hear her at first, and she had the chance to study him for a moment. Her heart sank as her eyes hungrily devoured the sight of him, so relaxed and sexy. She could feel her shaky willpower growing weaker by the moment.

Derek looked up and smiled at her, his eyes heart-wrenchingly tender behind his glasses. "Hi. Feel better?"

"Yes," she whispered, moistening her lips. She tried to strengthen her fading voice. "I'm sorry I went to sleep for so long."

"You needed the rest. Are you hungry?"

"Yes, I am, but—"

"Good. I've got dinner ready to go under the broiler. Nothing fancy, just ham, cheese and tomato open-faced sandwiches. Sound okay?"

"Definitely okay," she agreed with a touch of shyness. Her eyes seemed to have become fixed on the open collar of his close-fitting knit shirt, fascinated by the silky dark curls nestling there. She knew how hard his body felt through his clothes. Would he feel as hard without them? she wondered dreamily. She should make every effort *not* to find out. But already her fingers were twitching to test him.

Dinner was consumed in near silence, though Summer could have sworn she could hear her own heartbeat booming through the room. A new note of intimacy had been introduced into their relationship that day, and now she was aware, as she had not been before, of being truly alone with him. She sensed every movement he made, found herself incredibly attuned to his breathing and deep voice. Though the sandwiches were good, she found she could barely taste her food. Instead, she found herself avidly watching him eating his, finding the experience amazingly erotic. She'd never really thought eating was sexy, despite the books she'd read, but now she was beginning to understand. Each time Derek's mouth closed around his sandwich, she shivered, imagining those lips on her skin.

*Dammit, stop this!* she told herself desperately. *Say something! Anything!*

"This is the second time you've made dinner for me, Derek," she said at last, as if he couldn't remember that vitally important fact for himself. "I'll have to return the favor sometime."

*Really dumb, Reed,* she scolded herself. *Why didn't you just ask the guy for a date?*

"I'm not much of a chef," Derek admitted. "I've served you my entire repertoire of dishes now. Steaks and sandwiches."

"Both of which have been excellent."

"Thank you. Do you like to cook, Summer?"

"Sometimes. Nothing fancy, though. Connie says that I cook with an Arkansas accent."

"Meaning?"

"Just that I cook like a rural Southern housewife— the way my mother cooks, to be precise. Plain meats, potatoes and gravy, vegetables boiled with pork seasoning. California nutritionists would be appalled at the amount of calories and carbohydrates and cholesterol, or whatever, but the food tastes good, and that kind of cooking has raised generations of healthy Reeds and Welches."

"Welch was your mother's maiden name?"

"Yes. Amazing what little tidbits you're finding out about me, isn't it?"

"There are still a lot of things I want to know," he replied.

Summer shook her head. "No more of my life history. I'm bored with the subject. I'd rather talk about you tonight."

"Now that's a boring subject." Derek gathered his supper dishes and carried them into the kitchen, leaving Summer to assume that the conversation had been brought to an abrupt end. She sighed in exasperation and reached for her own plate.

"How's your leg?" Derek asked when they were seated on the oatmeal-colored sofa in the den, two cups of coffee on the low table in front of them.

"Fine. Tell me about your work, Derek."

He refused to take the hint. "It's throbbing, isn't it?"

"Your work? Interesting, perhaps, but hardly—"

"Summer." He put the palm of his hand firmly over her mouth. "Your leg. Does it hurt?"

"A little," she mumbled behind his hand, glaring at him.

Derek nodded shortly and dropped his hand. "I think I prefer the other way of shutting you up," he told her, his eyes glinting silver with his smile. "With a kiss."

Summer privately decided that she preferred that method, as well, but she chose to keep that thought to herself.

Derek patted his lap. "Put your leg up here. I'll massage it for you."

"Oh, I don't—"

"Dammit, woman. Must you argue with everything I say?" he roared. "Give me the damned leg!"

Summer gave him the damned leg. "You're so bossy," she accused him resentfully.

Derek's long fingers began to work magic on her aching knee. "And you're so stubborn. Why did you push yourself so hard this afternoon? Your leg started hurting almost an hour before the rehearsal was over, didn't it?"

She sighed. "It was the Cyndi Lauper dance," she confessed. "I got a little carried away."

"Why didn't you stop? You could have rested for a few minutes."

She shrugged. "If you take a break with those kids, you're liable to lose them entirely. I didn't want to risk messing up a great rehearsal. Wasn't it terrific? There wasn't even a major fight among the performers this time. Some of the kids really show talent, don't you think?"

"They're not bad," Derek conceded, watching her face as he continued to massage the slender leg in his lap. His fingers were warm through the soft denim, and the tense muscles under them were slowly beginning to relax. "But you were the one with the talent."

Summer found herself contending with conflicting sensations. Derek's skillful massage was wonderful, the all too familiar ache in her leg receding under its effect with magical speed. Yet the movement of those long fingers on her thigh and knee were bringing another kind of ache deep in her abdomen, an ache that threatened to be infinitely more serious than the twinges of an old injury. Infinitely more dangerous. "Uh, thank you," she said, remembering that he'd complimented her. *Concentrate on the conversation,* she ordered herself sternly.

"It's really a shame that you abandoned your talent when you had the accident," Derek commented, still watching her face for a reaction.

"Oh, I think the entertainment world is surviving without me," Summer returned lightly. "Tell me about your travels with your government job, Derek. It must have been fascinating seeing all those different parts of the world."

"Hotel rooms and smoke-filled offices look pretty much the same everywhere," he replied, using the stock answer that he'd been throwing out for the past ten years or so. He had become an expert on evading questions about his former line of work simply by making it sound too dull to discuss. "You're good with kids. Have you ever thought of teaching theater arts to young people?"

"You're good with open-faced sandwiches. Have you ever thought about becoming a short-order cook?"

Summer almost flinched from the look of anger that Derek turned her way. "Will you take nothing seriously?" he demanded. "Don't you ever get tired of turning every statement into a stupid joke?"

"Don't you ever get tired of giving advice to other people about how they should conduct their lives?" she retorted evenly. "I'm not one of your clients, Derek. I haven't hired you to offer your valuable services. Save it for the businessmen who *want* to hear it."

"So you're perfectly content drifting along the way you have been, working in a job you dislike, donating a few hours of your time to good causes, wasting the rest of your life playing games and making jokes?" His fingers had ceased their soothing motion and were gripping her leg in a white-knuckled clench that clearly expressed his frustration.

"Yes!" she answered hotly. "Face it, Derek. I'm exactly the shallow, empty-headed party girl you've thought I was all along. I know you've hated admitting that you might actually be attracted to such a person and you've tried to find a frustrated career woman inside me. It's time for you to realize that she isn't there. I'm exactly what you see, and I have no desire to be anything else."

"You are a fraud, Summer Reed." Derek's voice was cold as he lifted her leg from his lap to set it with care in front of her.

She immediately scooted back to put more space between them, watching him warily. "What do you mean?"

"Just what I said. You're a fraud. A fake. An actress putting on a twenty-four-hour-a-day performance. You act like an airhead hedonist to hide the fact that you were devastated by the accident that left you lame and took away your hopes of a career in entertainment. You continue to find dead-end jobs because you know there's nothing you really want to do other than sing and dance and act. If you can't have that, you don't want anything. Right?

"You pretend that your hours with the kids at Halloran House are just a favor to your buddy Clay, not anything that brings you fulfillment. You keep avoiding serious relationships with men on the pretext of looking for a nonexistent hero, when the truth is that you're scared. Because one jerk couldn't deal with your physical imperfection, you assume that no other man could, either."

"Stop it!" Summer shouted, appalled. Her eyes were a brilliant blue in a face that had gone white. "Who the hell asked for your opinion of me, Derek Anderson? What gives you the right to act like you know me so well?"

"Because I do," he answered implacably. "I've watched you, Summer. I've read the shadows in your eyes, the expressions that crossed your face when you thought no one was looking. I saw the wistfulness there when your friends abandoned you in a corner while they danced at your party. I saw the courage it took for you to circulate with the people you didn't know at my party, the tiny spasms of pain whenever one of my guests would innocently inquire about your limp. And I saw the sheer joy in your beautiful eyes this afternoon when you were working with those kids, singing and dancing and performing."

Summer clasped her hands in front of her in an exaggerated show of amazement. "Derek, that's incredible!" she jeered. "How long have you been a mind reader? You should work up a nightclub act, and I could be your assistant since I'm nurturing all these hidden desires to perform that you've told me about."

"Dammit, Summer, stop it!" he shouted, dropping his hands on her shoulders and clenching his fingers as if he'd like nothing more than to shake some sense into her. "Can't you stop joking even long enough to get mad at me? Curse at me or hit me or something, but stop hiding what you're feeling behind this idiotic clown act!"

Summer felt something break inside her head, releasing a torrent of emotions that had been safely dammed for a long time. With the flood came an outpouring of words, furious and twisted and tumbling as they flowed from her mouth almost against her will. "What do you want from me, Derek? Do you want me to fall apart and sob into your shoulder about the cruel trick life played on me? All right, dammit!

"I hated waking up in a hospital with a bloody pulp where there had once been a pretty nice-looking leg! I hated the fear I felt when the doctors told me they might have to amputate! I hated the pain that was so excruciating that I screamed and cried and begged for drugs to make me sleep so that I wouldn't feel it! I hated having the man I thought I loved look at me with pity, then tell me that he couldn't deal with an invalid!

"I hated those months in bed, and the operations that left me with more artificial parts in my leg than real ones. I hated being in a wheelchair. I hated the walker and the crutches. The exercises that hurt like hell yet were necessary if I ever wanted to walk again. And I hated knowing that for the rest of my life people will look at me with pity for the poor, crippled woman!"

Derek did shake her then, though gently. "Look at me, Summer," he commanded her, holding her only inches away from him. "Look at my face. Do you see pity there? I said *look at me!*"

Tear-washed blue eyes tentatively searched his face. She saw the remains of anger there, and a pain that she wasn't sure she understood. She ran her eyes slowly across his dark face, her gaze lingering on his emotion-darkened gray eyes. Anger, pain, desire, frustration— but not pity. Even after all she'd just told him. "No," she whispered, remembering that he'd asked her a question. "I don't see pity."

"Summer, there is so much more to you than a quick wit and a fast mouth and a lame leg. Do you really think any of your true friends care whether you walk with a limp or would think any less of you if you carried on a serious conversation without cracking jokes? I know you love to laugh, and you've probably always been a tease and a cutup, but don't hide your other nice qualities. Give people a chance to get to know the real you— fears and disappointments and insecurities and all. Nobody expects you to be perfect."

Summer looked wonderingly at him for a long moment before dropping her head to stare at her lap. "When I was little, I learned that people love to be entertained," she said quietly, almost surprising herself at what she was saying. Derek shifted on the sofa beside her but remained quiet, encouraging her to continue as if he knew that the explanation she was about to make was important to both of them.

"My older sister, Spring, was smart and serious and everyone admired her, and Autumn was the baby— beautiful and spunky and tough, which earned her respect at an early age. I could make people laugh. I could sing and dance and do imitations, and people enjoyed my performances. I thrived on the applause and the approval."

She cleared her throat. "I found out that people are uncomfortable with the pain and fears of others, but everyone loves to share a good joke. So I hid my fears and insecurities and I always had friends. Sometimes I wished that I had someone I could cry with or tell my problems to, but I was afraid my friends wouldn't **have** liked me as well if I stopped making them laugh."

"It wouldn't have mattered to your real friends," he told her softly.

"Perhaps." She didn't sound convinced. She glanced up at him, then as quickly looked away. "I was quite popular in college. The other kids admired me because I didn't seem to care whether I passed or failed while they sweated through classes in fear. I did care, of course, but I didn't want anyone to know—just in case I failed. If they thought it was because I didn't care, they wouldn't think of it as failure, I thought.

"I had such big dreams. Few people knew the number of hours I spent practicing my dancing and my singing and my acting. I pictured myself as a star with constant applause and thousands of friends and fans. Then I met Lonnie."

"The boyfriend? 'Enry 'Iggins?''

She didn't smile. "Yes. He was gorgeous. And he had talent. I thought the two of us together would be a team to take the country by storm. He thought so, too. I don't know if we were in love with each other or with our mutual dreams of stardom. And then I had the accident." She swallowed. "He was so angry with me."

Derek looked startled. "Angry?"

She nodded. "For ruining everything. He never did like me taking the motorcycle out on the streets—said it was too dangerous for a dancer. When I proved him right, he wouldn't forgive me for taking the risk. He told me that a crippled girlfriend would hold him back, that he needed someone who could share his life in every way."

"Bastard."

"Yeah, well, anyway, those first few days after the accident were pretty grim. The pain and the knowledge that my dancing days were over made it hard for me to be brave. All I could do was cry. My friends didn't quite know what to do with me. They visited me, of course, but it was easy to see that they were uncomfortable and they felt sorry for me. I hated that. So I forced myself to smile and built up a repertoire of gimp jokes. Pretty soon my friends were flocking back around me, telling me how brave and wonderful I was."

"What about your family?"

Her face softened. "Bless their hearts, they were wonderful. They might not have understood me all the time. Maybe they didn't know quite how much my dancing meant to me, but they knew I was in pain and bitterly disappointed and they rallied round me. My sisters were there to let me cry into their shoulders, and my mother bullied me into doing the exercises even when they hurt, then kissed me when I cried. My father put me straight to work to give me something to concentrate on besides my problems. I had to be careful not to become too dependent on them all."

"Which is the reason you moved to San Francisco?"

"Yes. I had to prove to myself and to them that I was capable of functioning on my own. And I have. Even though they, like you, aren't all that thrilled with the way I've chosen to live."

"Perhaps they don't approve, but do they pity you?" Derek asked perceptively.

"Why, no," Summer answered, surprised that he would ask, "of course they don't pity me. They love me."

"Even though they've seen you at your lowest point, and they've heard you cry and curse and feel sorry for yourself?" he asked quietly.

She grimaced at him. "Another object lesson, Derek?"

"Merely an observation."

She squirmed uncomfortably on the couch. "I don't know why I always end up telling you my life story," she told him accusingly.

"I know you think I'm interfering and nosy, but I can't help it," Derek confessed. "I'm not usually like this outside of business."

"How did Connie and I get so lucky?" Summer asked dryly.

A touch of red darkened his high cheekbones, startling Summer. "Connie's my sister," he muttered. "I love her, and I want what's best for her. And you, well, I...I like you," he said with an uncharacteristic stammer. "It bothers me to see you hiding your pain and your feelings from the people who care for you."

Summer's own cheeks were suspiciously warm. "I've never even talked to Connie the way I just talked to you," she admitted in a very low voice, almost a whisper. "I don't know why I've been able to tell you things that I couldn't tell anyone else."

"Maybe because I've insisted," Derek suggested wryly.

She smothered a nervous giggle. "That might have something to do with it." She risked an atypically shy glance at him and found her eyes held by his. She found it hard to read the expression she saw deep in the pewter-gray depths. Had discovering her weaknesses changed the way Derek perceived her? Was he disappointed that she wasn't as strong and tough as she'd pretended? Did he . . . did he still want her?

Suddenly she had to know. She couldn't come right out and ask, but she could find out another way. "Would you . . . would you hold me, Derek?" she asked hesitantly. "Just for a little while?"

# 9

WITHOUT EVEN a momentary hesitation Derek took Summer into his arms. Folded against his wide, hard chest, Summer released a breath that she hadn't known she'd been holding and snuggled into his strength. She felt his heart beating steadily against her cheek through the soft knit fabric of his white pullover. In only moments she felt the heartbeat speed up, just as her own was doing. Her arms went around Derek's lean waist.

His hands moved on her back, tentatively at first, then more demandingly. Finally one hand moved up the back of her head, fingers threading through the short, silky hair there as he tilted her head back. They both felt her tremor as she turned her face up to his in mute invitation. He kissed her with a force that was surprisingly gentle, considering the fire and passion it incited in her.

"Derek. Oh, Derek." Summer pulled her arms from around his waist to throw them around his neck.

"Summer." Derek's voice was so hoarse that neither of them recognized it. "I want you so much it's driving me mad."

She believed him. Derek didn't pity her. He was not repelled by her scars or her awkward limp. He wanted her. As he pulled her rather roughly against him, she was made physically aware of just how much he wanted her. And she wanted him. Her fingers slid into the crisp hair at the back of his neck, curling there to bring his mouth down to hers.

Her eyes locked with his, she brushed her mouth across his lips, then back again. She felt the sudden stillness that gripped him, tensing his muscles against her. He waited, seemingly without breathing, as she drew back fractionally and then kissed him again, bolder now. The tip of her tongue slipped out to taste him. Derek's short, dark lashes swept downward to hide the glitter of his eyes from her for just a moment before his feverish gaze locked once again with hers. That moment was long enough for her to recognize his vulnerability. Amazingly enough, Derek seemed unsure what to do next.

It was his uncharacteristic hesitation that removed the last vestiges of her own doubt. "I want you, Derek," she whispered, her lips like wisps of smoke against his.

"Summer?" His voice was raw.

"Yes, Derek. Please."

He gave a little sound that was half groan and half exultant laugh. As if he were afraid she'd change her mind, he swept her into his arms and off the couch before she was quite aware of what was happening. She put her arms trustingly around his neck, enjoying the feeling of being carried in the arms of the man who was about to become her lover.

Her lover. The thought made her go so weak that, had she been trying to walk, she would have fallen. She had never wanted another man this much.

Depositing her carefully on the geometric-print bedspread that covered a massive king-size bed, Derek began to tug at her white fleece top even as she reached for the band of his own white knit shirt. Both felt the need to touch and explore, and it was not necessary for them to put their desire into words. They communicated with their eyes and their lips, with husky little moans and breathless laughs, and when small, soft breasts were pressed at last to broad, plated chest, their delirious sighs sounded in stereo in the shadowed room.

"God, you feel good," Derek groaned, sliding sensuously against her.

"So do you," she whispered in response, feeling her breasts tighten and harden in delicious response.

He kissed her throat, then lower, moving toward those pebbled tips that so craved his attention. "You're protected?" he questioned suddenly, lifting his head for a moment to look at her in concern. "If not, I can—"

"It's okay, Derek," she assured him quickly, her fingers tangling in his hair. "I'm protected." Her taste for adventure did not preclude taking certain precautions, a habit for which she was now very grateful.

Derek's murmur signified his own relief that there was nothing to hold him back from finally satisfying his hunger for her. He lowered his head once more.

Summer rapidly discovered that Derek's talent at kissing was only a hint of his skill as a lover. From the short, tousled strands of her amber-brown hair to the hollows of her ears and throat, from her flushed, swollen breasts to the delicate indentation of her navel, from the silky curves of her inner thighs to the ticklish arches of her feet, he explored and pleasured so thoroughly that Summer was a writhing, moaning creature of pure sensation by the time he lost his own tenuous control.

Moments before she couldn't have imagined it was possible for the pleasure to intensify. Now, with her legs wrapped tightly around his lean hips, his fingers biting into the soft flesh of her buttocks, Summer discovered that there were heights of passion that she had never dreamed existed. Arching into his driving thrusts, she responded wholeheartedly to his every movement, drawing moans of delight from him in answer to her own.

Her head tossing on the pillow, she arched again to draw him even deeper into her. "Oh, Derek," she whispered brokenly.

"Summer. So good," he moaned, the words hot against her throat.

She tried to tell him that it was good for her, too, but the words shattered into a cry of joyous release as tiny ripples swelled into pounding waves of fulfillment. Dimly aware of the shudders that rocked Derek's body within the cradle of her arms and legs, she smiled in exhausted satisfaction, then collapsed beneath him with a long, audible sigh.

Lying heavily on top of her, Derek knew he'd have to move, but he wondered where he'd ever find the strength. It seemed to take everything he had left when he finally made himself roll to one side to relieve her slight body of his weight, though he didn't take his arms from around her. "God," he groaned after a few more moments of recovery. "I think I died."

His words provoked a breathless little laugh from the woman in his arms. "You, too?" she asked in a gasp. "I feel like I've melted into a puddle all over your lovely bedspread."

She squirmed around to face him, lifting herself on one elbow. Smiling down at him, she reached out to brush a strand of dark hair away from his forehead. Her lover, she thought again, and this time the words were fact.

He lifted one hand to touch her cheek. "I wanted you so much that I went a little crazy. I didn't hurt you, did I?"

She smiled and kissed his palm. "No, you didn't hurt me."

"How's your leg?"

"Deliriously happy."

He chuckled and pulled her down against his chest. "Lie still a moment," he ordered her indulgently. "I need some recovery time."

"Mmm." She snuggled her cheek into the hollow of his shoulder and idly caressed his chest through the swirls of dark hair. Her eyes closed in pure contentment, she allowed herself to drift, holding serious thought at bay. She was not quite ready to consider the change that had just come about in her life—and she knew the change was a momentous one. No, for now she wanted only to bask in the security of Derek's arms. Her eyes opened halfway and her gaze wandered idly around his bedroom, narrowing a little as she took in the assorted trophies and sports pictures with which he had chosen to decorate. Even that discovery was pushed quickly to the back of her mind. No thoughts of physical handicaps or other differences between them were to be allowed to intrude on her euphoria.

As if to block any further observations, her eyes closed again, firmly. She wouldn't have believed that she would be able to sleep again so soon after her nap, but the deep, even rhythm of Derek's breathing soon lulled her into a light dream state, a soft smile gracing her flushed features.

The line between dream and reality wavered and languorously dissolved. A tiny sound of pleasure flowed from Summer's slightly parted lips as she felt her heavy-limbed body being thoroughly and leisurely caressed. Arching like a lazy cat into the gently arousing strokes, she opened luminous eyes to study Derek's face, so close to her own.

His face would never look soft, but it held more warmth now than she had ever imagined seeing there. His eyes gleamed silver, his mouth had relaxed its stern lines into a semismile. Fascinated by the way his dark, disheveled hair was beginning to curl at his forehead— *so that's why he keeps it so short*, she thought in tender amusement—she drank in the sight of him. He looked approachable, she mused, reaching up to touch his lean cheek. He looked wonderful. "I take it you've recovered?" she murmured huskily.

He kissed the soft upper slope of her breast. "Umm."

She took that to be an affirmative. "Oh, good." Her drawl turned to a gasp as his tongue darted out to circle her already distended nipple, and then he was pulling the dusky peak into the liquid warmth of his mouth. Summer moaned her approval and threaded her fingers into his hair to hold him closer.

Derek's hand slid down her side, pausing to trace each rib. She squirmed, offering her other breast to his worshipful mouth. Her attention alternated between the manipulations of his lips, teeth and tongue, and his slowly descending hand, which was shaping her hips.

She stiffened fractionally when his exploring fingers slid down her leg and touched the ridges of her scars. How could he not be repulsed by them?

Misinterpreting her tension, Derek lifted his mouth from her moistened nipple to kiss her chin. "I won't hurt you," he whispered against her lips.

"I know. It's not that," she assured him. "It's just—"

She stopped by necessity when his mouth covered hers. Even as he kissed her with a hunger that was unabated by their recent lovemaking, Derek cupped her impaired knee, his fingers tender, soothing. Uncertain of what message to read into his actions, Summer reached down to capture his wrist and pull his hand to her breast. Again she had chosen not to linger on thoughts that threatened to dim her present pleasure.

Complying with her unspoken request, Derek concentrated on rebuilding her arousal. Summer responded eagerly to his skillful attentions, her own fingers dancing across his sleek back. When his hand moved downward again, it was only as far as the damp nest of curls between her thighs, where the bud of her femininity quivered beneath his touch.

Her breath catching in ragged gasps, Summer arched again and again into his palm, her mouth seeking and finding his. He moved between her legs, and she stopped breathing entirely, anxiously awaiting the moment when he would once again make them one.

And then he murmured something that stopped her heart along with her breathing.

"I love you, Summer."

"*What?*"

His hand on his chest, Derek stared at the woman who'd leaped straight up to sit on the bed beside him and was staring openmouthed back at him. "God, Summer, you almost gave me a heart attack. Why did you shriek at me like that?"

"What did you say?"

"I said you scared the—"

"No, before that."

"Oh." His face relaxed into a smile. "I said I love you."

"Oh, my God." She covered her face with her hands.

Though his body still quivered with his arousal, Derek laughed under his breath and reached for her wrists. "I should have known your reaction wouldn't be the traditional 'I love you, too, Derek.' But I had no idea I'd have to peel you off the ceiling once my heart started beating again. Is it that much of a shock, Summer-love?"

Her hands completely limp in his, Summer gaped at him. "A shock? Yes, Derek, I guess you could call it a shock." She sounded stunned.

"Why? Couldn't you see it coming? I've suspected it for some time. I've never been in love before, but I'm not so dense that I didn't recognize the emotion when it hit me."

"How could I have seen it coming?" she asked spiritedly. "My God, Derek, we've only known each other a week."

"A week and two days. Not that it matters. I wanted you from the first moment I saw you sitting on that rickety stool in your apartment. I think I fell in love with you the first time I kissed you, though I was mad enough at that moment to strangle you."

She couldn't believe he was saying these things, not Derek. She'd known he wanted her, of course. But love? How could he tell her so calmly that he loved her, when she was certain that such an admission could not come easily to a reserved, careful man like Derek?

Searching her face, Derek stopped, his smile fading. "Maybe I've been taking too much for granted. I thought you were feeling the same way I was. Was I wrong, Summer?"

"I . . ." She let her voice trail off and dropped her eyes to hide her fear and confusion. "Derek, you can't be in love with me. I'm not anything like the women you've dated before."

He groaned. "Don't start that again. I was never in love with any of the women I dated before. How could I have known what kind of woman I could fall in love with before I met you? I wasn't even sure it was possible for me to fall in love. And then I fell head over heels for a smart mouth and the most beautiful blue eyes I've ever seen." Before she could form a reply, his fingers tightened around her wrist in what she could almost believe was a surge of desperation.

"Summer, I love you. I can't give you logical explanations or reasonable excuses, but I know it's true. How do you feel about me?"

Avoiding his intense scrutiny, her eyes focused painfully on a framed photograph of Derek breaking the tape in a marathon race, his arms lifted in triumph above his head, healthy legs shown to perfection beneath his brief running shorts. "Derek, we need time," she whispered. "It's too soon. You—we can't be sure."

"Oh."

The single syllable was stark enough to make her risk a quick look at his face. Derek was so good at hiding his feelings, but somehow she had learned to read him quite accurately in the past nine days. Only she could have seen that she had hurt him. She felt as if she'd plunged a knife into her own heart.

"Derek, you don't understand. I care for you, of course I do, but—"

"But I'm no hero, right?" he finished tonelessly. "I'm still just Connie's brother, Derek, the stuffed-shirt businessman who happens to kiss well enough to entice you into bed."

The knife twisted. "That's not what I was going to say."

"Listen to me, Summer Reed." He caught her chin between his thumb and forefinger, lifting her face until his stormy gray eyes were boring directly into hers. "I'll give you time if you need it, but I'm not giving up. I love you like no fairy-tale hero could ever love you, and I know you better than anyone else ever has. You don't stand a chance against me. I have a reputation for achieving my goals, and you are my priority-one goal from now on. Do you understand?"

He had barked out the words in a militarily autocratic tone that automatically stiffened her spine. "I hear you, Derek."

"Good. Believe it." He leaned over to kiss her, hard, then released her. "Do you want me to take you home now?"

She wanted him to take her into his arms and make love to her. She wanted to allow herself to believe that he really loved her and that his infatuation would not go away when he tired of her erratic humor and offbeat life-style and her inability to keep up with him physically. She wanted to believe that her heart would not be permanently shattered when he moved on to someone else. She knew better. She'd thought Lonnie had hurt her when he'd turned away from her after the accident. She suspected now that she'd never known pain as she could know it if Derek were to love her for a time and then leave her.

No. She'd had too much pain. This time she had to protect herself.

"Yes, please, Derek. Take me home."

Hurt and anger dulled the silver in his eyes, but he only nodded and reached for his scattered clothing as she did the same.

Though he walked her to the door after the painfully silent drive, carrying the packages she'd so cheerfully loaded into his arms several momentous hours earlier, Derek refused to go inside the apartment. He explained that he was not in the mood to deal with Connie just then. He transferred her packages to her arms, making a visible effort not to touch her. "When can I see you again?" he asked, the question verging on demand.

Summer looked pleadingly at him. "Please, Derek. I really think y—we need time. It's happened too fast."

His face hard, he glared immovably down at her. "When, Summer?"

She sighed. He would not make it easy for her, she thought glumly. His mind was set. She'd just have to prove to him that they were not suited to each other, no matter how desperately she wished they were. Perhaps another weekend with her would bore him, make him restless for someone who could play tennis or run with him. It would rip her heart to shreds, but perhaps he'd finally see what she was trying to tell him. "Call me later in the week," she said finally. "Maybe next weekend—"

"Fine," he cut in shortly. For a moment she thought he was going to walk away without another word. But then he reached for her, and his voice was urgent when he spoke. "It was good for us tonight, wasn't it, Summer?"

Giving in to a momentary weakness, she dropped her packages unheeded to the floor and burrowed into his arms. "Oh, yes, Derek," she breathed, looking up at him with an expression that left no doubt of her sincerity. "It was wonderful."

"Better than anything that ever happened to me before. Remember that," he told her softly. "Remember the way we've been drawn together from the beginning, despite our unimportant differences. Remember that you've been able to tell me things about yourself that you've never shared with anyone else. There's more to what we have than sexual attraction, Summer, and you're bright enough to figure that out if you'll stop fighting it. I love you."

He kissed her long and hard, with undertones of the passion they had shared in his bed. And then he was gone.

Summer was breathing raggedly when she entered the apartment. Connie was sitting on the couch, the telephone cradled on her shoulder as she painted her long nails a bright fuchsia. She smiled at Summer in greeting. Summer tried to return the smile as she passed the couch to her room, where she closed the door, threw her packages on a chair and fell in a nerveless heap on the bed.

She hadn't bothered to turn on a light, so the darkness of her bedroom closed around her as she lay huddled in a position of abject misery. It was so utterly ironic, she thought bleakly. Derek had tried to convince her that she was in love with him. Little did he know that she needed no convincing. She knew full well that she loved Derek Anderson. Blindly, desperately, hopelessly, eternally. She'd never loved like this before, she'd never love like this again.

And he had said he loved her, too. She should be deliriously happy. Instead, she wanted nothing more than to die.

"Summer?" Connie cracked open the door and peeked inside when Summer did not respond to a light knock. "Why are you lying here in the dark with all your clothes on? What's wrong?"

"Nothing," Summer answered in a voice so thick with tears that it was obvious she was lying. "Everything."

Connie promptly walked inside, crossing the room to sit on the bed beside her unhappy roommate. "Do you want to talk about it? We're friends, Summer. We should be able to share the bad times as well as the good."

Summer mopped at her face with one hand, sorely tempted to pour the whole story into Connie's shoulder. But maybe Connie wouldn't want to hear her roommate's problems, she thought. After all, Connie probably had problems of her own. For the first time in her life Summer understood that, with all the friends she had attracted over the years with her playful, carefree humor, there had never been anyone she could cry with. Derek had forced her to admit that earlier; now she realized that it was really true.

"Summer, honey, what is it?" Connie had never seen Summer cry, just as she had never allowed herself to shed tears in front of her roommate. But, rather than being uncomfortable or impatient, as Summer might have feared, Connie reacted as a true friend, with a sympathetic desire to help. She reached out and touched Summer's shoulder. "Talk to me, Summer."

Without further hesitation Summer sat up and threw her arms around her friend—her *real* friend. "Oh,

Connie, I *do* want to talk about it," she moaned, the tears flowing freely.

"It's about Derek, isn't it? Believe me, I know how much his continuous criticism can hurt. I've come home and cried more than once. What did the creep say to hurt you?" Connie's voice had become more heated with each word.

Summer shook her head and swallowed a sob. "No, Connie, it wasn't that. He didn't criticize me."

Connie went still. "Oh, no." She gasped. "He didn't— Summer, did he—"

Realizing the direction of Connie's thoughts, Summer sat up straight in indignation. "Connie, he didn't hurt my physically, if that's what you're thinking. My God, he's your brother. You surely know him better than that."

Connie went limp with relief. "I thought I did," she admitted. "But where you're concerned, I don't know him at all. He's different with you."

The sob escaped. "I know," Summer whispered, covering her face with her hands. "Oh, Connie, what am I going to do?"

"You've fallen in love with him, haven't you?" Connie asked in surprise. "You've actually fallen in love with Derek."

"Yes," Summer whispered. "Are you very much surprised?"

"Maybe a little," Connie admitted with a short laugh. "I mean, you and Derek... Still, I've watched you with him. I've seen the way you treated other men during the time you and I have known each other. You wouldn't have let any of them boss you around like Derek does. And there was something in your eyes when you looked at him at his party last night, and again this morning when he came for you. It's in his eyes, too, you know."

"I know," Summer murmured.

"But if you're in love with him, I can see why you're so unhappy. I guess I've started to see that Derek's not quite the boring tyrant I've built him up to be during the past few months, but I don't know if he's capable of really loving a woman the way you'd want to be loved. He'd have to admit that he's as human as anyone else."

"Connie, he told me tonight that he loves me," Summer blurted out bravely.

Connie gazed wide-eyed at her friend. "He did?"

"Yes, he did."

"How? I mean, was he passionate and romantic and the whole bit?"

Summer chuckled despite her pain. "He was marvelous, Connie. Passionate and romantic and the whole bit."

"Wow." Connie shook her head in pleased amazement. "I knew you were good for him. So what's the problem? Why the tears?"

"That's why," Summer wailed. "He can't really be in love with me."

"Come on, Summer, Derek's not the type to lie to you just to get you into bed. One thing about my brother, he's honest. Too honest sometimes," she added with a wince. "If he says something, he means it."

"I know he thinks he's in love with me. He certainly wasn't telling me just to get me into bed. I was already there." Summer sighed. Rushing on when Connie lifted an eyebrow in interest, she continued, "I think he's been carried away with physical attraction, Connie. He's convinced himself that he's in love because it happened so fast and so intensely and he doesn't know how else to explain it. He's not giving himself enough time to be objective and look at the reasons why it just couldn't work."

"Summer, forgive me, but that's the dumbest thing I've ever heard," Connie said bluntly. "You act like he's an infatuated schoolboy. The man's pushing forty, Summer, and he has certainly had his share of women. I don't mean to offend you, my friend, but it's not like you're the type of woman who'd drive a man senseless with lust. You're cute and everything, but we're not talking Miss Universe here."

"Oh, Connie." Summer smiled through her tears. "Don't make me laugh now. Can't you see I'm trying to be miserable?"

"I can't help it. Derek would laugh, too, if he could hear what you're saying. I think he knows lust from love."

"But how could he be in love with me? He barely knows me, and he doesn't approve of what he does know."

"You're in love with him, and the situation is the same for you," Connie pointed out. "You haven't known him any longer, and he's hardly the hero you've been looking for. Come on, Summer, if anyone had told you a couple of weeks ago that you would fall for a somewhat stuffy, ultraconservative former bureaucrat, you'd have laughed in his face. Admit it."

"Well, yes, but Derek's not really like that, Connie. He has a great sense of humor; he just expresses it subtly. And he isn't all that proper when he's after something he really wants," she added, remembering the jeans and leather jacket and the incredibly adventurous lovemaking.

"Just as there is more to you than you'll allow most people to see," Connie said succinctly. "Obviously Derek has the intelligence and good sense to see beneath your eccentric exterior to find the common ground the two of you share."

"I'll admit that both Derek and I have sides to us that we don't normally put on display," Summer conceded. "But the parts of us that *are* visible are real, Connie, not deliberate misrepresentations. Derek really is a conservative businessman to whom things like schedules and responsibilities are important. And I truly enjoy the crazy parties we throw and the nutty friends that we've made and an occasional lapse into impulsive insanity. I'm terrified that Derek would try to change me into someone more like, well, like Joanne Payne. I'm afraid we'd start to hate each other, and I couldn't bear that."

"If he'd wanted Joanne Payne, he'd have kept her around. It's called compromise, Summer. It's part of any relationship between two naturally different individuals. That's why Stu and I didn't make it—because neither of us would give an inch. But you and Derek could do it, if you try. You give in on the things that are particularly important to him, and he does the same for you. You attend his boring, business-related cocktail parties, and he learns to enjoy himself at your bashes. You live on his schedule during the week, and he keeps the weekends open for impulsive adventures."

"Maybe." Though she didn't sound entirely convinced, Summer allowed that subject to drop. "There's something else," she murmured, looking down at her clenched hands. Without looking up she explained. "Do you think Derek has really stopped to think about what it would be like to be involved with a woman who couldn't join him in all those sports he loves so much?

You told me yourself when he was dating Joanne that you thought her backhand was the quality he most admired in her. I put myself on crutches for almost a month last year simply by playing a sedate game of volleyball. If Derek loves sports so much, he's going to want to continue to participate in them. And, while I wouldn't mind occasionally, I sure don't want to spend all my leisure time sitting on the sidelines. That may be selfish, but I can't help it. I'm a doer, Connie, not a watcher."

"Compromise," Connie reminded her. "You find things that you can do together. Like swimming. You've always been overly sensitive about your limp, Summer. It doesn't make that much difference to the people who care for you. Tell me, Summer, did you discuss these things with Derek tonight?"

"No," Summer admitted. "I ran. I just knew I had to give him time to be absolutely sure about his feelings for me."

"But you did tell him that you love him, didn't you?"

Summer squirmed. "No."

"Oh, great. He's probably as miserable as you are right now. Maybe he thinks you're the one who couldn't possibly love him, and you're trying to find a way to break it off gently."

*I'm no hero, right?* Derek had asked with pain in his deep voice. Summer winced as she realized how badly her instinctive rejection had hurt him after he'd opened up enough to tell her that he loved her. Especially after the lovemaking they'd just shared. *God, what a mess*, she moaned inwardly.

"Maybe you do need the time, Summer," Connie said gently. "Time to work out your fears. But don't shut Derek out. Talk to him like you've talked to me tonight. If you're going to work this out, you're going to have to do it together."

"Connie, when did you suddenly get so wise?" Summer asked with a watery smile. "And why are you pushing me into your brother's arms?"

Connie grinned. "Are you kidding? This is the best thing that ever happened to me. If you marry Derek, I'll have the world's greatest sister-in-law and you'll keep him so busy that he'll never find the time to rearrange my life for me. You'll be happy, Derek will be happy, my parents will be happy and I'll be happy. This is great!"

"Connie, you're dreaming, but thank you. I really needed to talk this out with someone."

"Anytime, kid."

"If you ever need a shoulder . . ."

Connie stood and sighed melodramatically. "Offer Wednesday night after my date with Joel. I might need it then."

"You think there's a chance that you and Joel could get serious?"

"Who knows? You and Derek are living proof that stranger things have happened."

Summer was almost surprised to hear herself laugh. "Thanks a lot, friend."

Connie paused in the doorway on her way out. "Would it hurt to call Derek and wish him sweet dreams? I hate to think of my big brother crying himself to sleep."

Summer laughed again, as she'd been meant to do, and watched Connie leave. She spent a few minutes in contemplation of true friendship before stripping off her jeans and top and pulling on a pale blue nightgown. The silky fabric felt especially sensuous against her skin still sensitized by Derek's lovemaking. The memories that flooded her mind made her tremble. She stared at the telephone on her nightstand. She reached for the receiver, pulled back, drew a deep breath and reached out again.

## 10

DEREK SOUNDED GUARDED when he answered his phone. He obviously knew Summer was the caller.

Now that she had him on the line, she wasn't sure what she'd wanted to say. "Derek, it's Summer," she told him after a short pause.

"I thought it might be," he answered, confirming her guess. "Are you okay?"

The concern in his voice made her blink back a rush of tears. She hadn't cried this much in five years, she told herself impatiently. "I'm fine, Derek. Are you?"

"I'm sitting here staring into a double Scotch and wondering if I should have refused to take you home tonight," he answered flatly. "I'd like to be holding you instead of this glass. What happened, Summer?"

"I panicked," she admitted softly. "I just panicked. Things got too serious, and I couldn't think of a joke to lighten the mood, so I ran."

"That's what I thought," he murmured. "Summer, why did you go to bed with me tonight?"

She couldn't speak for a moment as the words jammed in her throat, then she forced herself to answer. "That's why I called, Derek. There was something I wanted to tell you."

There was a pause, and then he spoke tonelessly, as if dreading her answer but wanting to get it over with. "What is it, Summer?"

How vulnerable he was, Summer thought in bemusement. As vulnerable as she. She had been unintentionally cruel to him tonight. "I forgot to tell you that I love you, Derek. I think I have from the beginning."

When the pause at the other end threatened to turn into minutes, she asked anxiously, "Derek, did you hear me?"

"I heard you, Summer," he finally answered. "Did you just realize this?"

"No. I knew it even before we made love. I just wouldn't admit it."

"Then why did you put me through hell tonight?" Derek demanded in frustration. "What are you doing there when you should be here, in my bed? I thought you were trying to let me down easy because you didn't love me and didn't think you ever could."

"Derek, I never knew I could love anyone like this. But I still think you need time," she added hastily.

"Me? You were giving *me* time?" he asked incredulously. "Summer, I know how I feel. I'm not confused by my feelings for you. Forgive me for being blunt, darling, but I've known physical desire before and I've never confused great sex for anything more than it was. Tonight wasn't sex, Summer. Tonight was love."

"Oh, Derek, I want so much to believe that. I still think you should take time to think about what a relationship with me would involve. It would take compromise and lots of time because we really are different in some ways. I *am* lame, and I just can't promise that I'll be on time to everything or plan my days or weeks according to some schedule or—"

"Summer." Derek interrupted her gently, his voice sounding considerably lighter than it had when he'd answered the telephone. "Do you love me?"

"Yes, Derek, I love you."

"Then we'll work it out," he told her confidently. "Dammit, Summer, why didn't you stay and talk to me instead of leaving me to think you didn't love me?"

"I'm sorry."

"You should be. I don't know if I'm going to spank you or throw you to the floor and ravish you the next time I see you."

"Do I have a choice?" she asked with an attempt at humor.

"No. I think I'll let you worry about it. You deserve it. Will I see you tomorrow?"

Summer took a deep breath. "No, Derek. I still want you to take this week to think about us. Think about everything I've said and whether it's worth it to you to make some sacrifices and compromises. If you decide that I'm not right for you after all, I'll . . . I'll try to understand." She'd die, she thought, but she didn't voice that glum thought.

Derek growled very distinctly into the receiver. "You are driving me slowly insane, Summer Reed. The biggest obstacle I can see between us right now is your stubborn refusal to give me a chance to convince you that we can overcome the other obstacles. I'll take the damned week if you insist, but it's not going to change a thing. I'm old enough and experienced enough to know what I'm feeling and to understand what is involved here. Dammit, woman, I love you, and I'm going to convince you of that if it kills us both."

Summer laughed softly, reluctantly. "I'm beginning to believe you."

"Good. I'm the guy who always gets what he's after, remember?"

"I love you, Derek."

"I love you, Summer. Let me prove it to you."

"I'll talk to you next weekend," she promised and hung up the phone. When she went to sleep several hours later, it was with the hope that she and Derek did have a chance.

DEREK STARED DOWN at the phone, placed his glass of Scotch very carefully on the table beside it and stood motionless for a full minute. Then he suddenly punched the air above his head with one fist. "Yeah!" he yelled.

She loved him. Summer Reed loved him. High on a burst of sheer adrenaline, he was as exhilarated as he'd ever been after winning a marathon. His heart was pounding, his chest tight. She loved him. God, he felt good!

But how could she have walked away from him tonight after the most incredible lovemaking that he'd ever experienced? She had ripped him apart when she'd turned away from him after he'd told her he loved her. Maybe he'd been an arrogant jerk to assume she loved him simply because he loved her, but he could not imagine that she could respond to him the way she did and not care for him. And then she had closed her door in his face.

It had hurt. He hadn't known anything could hurt that much. But she loved him. That knowledge erased the pain as if it had never existed. Thank God she had called.

Imagine her thinking that their unimportant diversities would keep them apart. He knew they had their differences. Did she think he was so dense he didn't realize there would be compromises and sacrifices to make? There were some adjustments to make in any relationship that was worth pursuing. He could handle it. Summer was worth anything. But how could he convince her that he knew what he was doing?

Damn that spineless, self-centered actor who had walked out on her when she'd needed him. No wonder she was afraid to trust Derek's emotions now. What was it about charming, shallow actors that his sister and Summer had both been attracted to them in their pasts? Now Derek had to repair the damage. But how? How could he convince her that they weren't all that different?

He stood in deep contemplation for a while, then snapped his fingers. The grin that split his tanned face would have astonished his sister. It was an expression of pure mischief. Derek had a plan.

THE FLOWERS ARRIVED at her desk on Monday morning, a dozen red roses in an exquisite crystal vase. As the other women in the accounting department drooled in envy and her no-nonsense supervisor, Mr. Gleason, glowered at the distraction, Summer ripped open the card with fingers that displayed a disturbing tendency to tremble.

She knew right away that the bold, slashing script belonged to Derek, though the card was not signed.

You want romance? I'll give you romance. I love you.

"Wow," Connie breathed, coming from behind her desk to reverently touch the velvety petal of one perfect rose. "Oh, wow."

Summer hesitated for a moment, then handed Connie the card. She had to share what she was feeling with someone. Connie read the card in awe, then looked up to shake her head and repeat, "Oh, wow."

Summer took a deep breath and laughed shakily. "That's exactly the way I would have put it."

"This is so romantic. I can't believe Derek did this. How can you resist this?"

"I can't. And he knows it, the rat."

Connie laughed as Summer shook her head in exasperation.

"ANDERSON." Derek's voice over the telephone was clipped.

"Derek? It's Summer."

His voice softened. "Oh, hi, sweetheart. Did you get the roses?"

"Yes, and they're beautiful. But you're not playing fair."

"Hey, we never set any conditions about this week. I promised to give you time, but I never said I'd let you forget about me."

"I hardly think I'm going to forget you, Derek."

"You're not kidding. I've gotta go, sweetheart. I love you." He hung up before she could answer.

Derek smiled down at the telephone in satisfaction. He'd mapped out a precise campaign for the upcoming week, all carefully thought out to convince Summer that he was the man of her dreams. His siege had been planned as carefully as any mission he'd ever undertaken.

Once again the thought momentarily occurred to him that he should have told Summer the truth about the past, but still there was a reluctance to risk impressing her with a distorted image of a life of danger and adventure. No, better to leave it alone for now.

That would make her eventual surrender to him all the sweeter.

Thinking of the delivery he planned for her to receive the next day, Derek grinned wickedly. He'd almost forgotten how to play during the past few years, he mused. The sights he'd seen in Vietnam and in back alleys across Europe and the Middle East had been grim enough to drive the laughter out of even the most lighthearted of men. But Summer had given him back the ability to laugh and the urge to play. He could love her for that, even if he did not already adore her for her sweetness, her warmth and her kindness.

Derek pushed a button on his telephone and leaned close to the speaker. "Miss Barrett, get my travel agent on the phone for me, please."

ON TUESDAY a ragged bicycle messenger brought a thick manila envelope into the accounting department. Mr. Gleason looked more disapproving than ever when Connie immediately jumped up and rushed to Summer's desk. "Well?" she demanded. "What is it?"

"I don't know. I'm almost afraid to look." Summer carefully peeled back the flap. The envelope was filled with travel brochures. Brightly colored, glossy booklets extolling the virtues of the Bahamas, Japan, China, Australia, Southern France, Italy, India and more. A plain white card bore Derek's distinctive handwriting.

You want adventure? Tell me when you want to leave.

"I think I'm going to cry," Connie wailed when she read the card.

"Do that and Gleason will fire us on the spot," Summer protested, blinking back her own tears.

"I guess you're right. But it really is sweet, Summer."

"Yes," she whispered dreamily. "It really is sweet."

Derek wasn't playing fair at all.

ANOTHER ENVELOPE CAME on Wednesday. Mr. Gleason was heard to utter a rare curse when half the accounting department gathered around Summer's desk to watch her open it. Her heart pounding in her throat, Summer smiled tremulously at Connie and ripped open the envelope. Then shook it. Then pulled it apart and stared into it.

"It's empty," she concluded finally, looking up in bewilderment.

"It's empty?" everyone repeated in disappointed unison.

"He must have forgotten to put whatever it was in the envelope before he sealed it," Connie said slowly. "Though goodness knows that doesn't sound like Derek."

Summer pursed her lips and frowned thoughtfully at the torn package. "No," she said finally. "Derek didn't forget to put anything inside. This envelope was meant to be delivered empty. Just don't anyone ask me why. I have no idea."

"You mean," asked one of the women nearby, who had always found Summer and Connie thoroughly amusing, "some guy paid a fortune for a bicycle messenger to deliver an empty envelope?"

"I think so," Summer agreed.

The woman giggled. "Can you beat that? I always knew that you'd fall for someone as funny and unpredictable as you are, Summer."

The women went back to their desks, delighted with the unusual romance being carried on in their normally routine workdays.

Connie and Summer stared at each other for a moment, then burst into helpless laughter.

THE ROOMMATES RUSHED home from work Wednesday afternoon, both in a frenzy to get ready for their respective appointments. Munching on a peanut butter sandwich, Summer stripped out of the sweater and skirt she'd worn to the office and pulled on a purple-and-yellow-printed knit shirt and a pair of baggy yellow overalls. Then she began to look around her bedroom for the notes she'd need during the final rehearsal of the Halloran House talent show. Naturally, the papers were nowhere to be found.

"Dammit!" she muttered, heedlessly trashing the tiny writing desk in one corner of the bedroom. "Where are those notes?" Paperback romances and leather-bound classics fell into a heap on the carpet, followed by an oversize pictorial history of musical comedy movies and a *Cosmopolitan* magazine.

When the desk failed to produce the papers she needed, Summer groaned and began to go through a stack of magazines on the floor beside her bed.

"Summer! I can't find my red knit dress. Do you have any suggestions where it might be?" Connie's voice from the other room sounded frantic.

"It's at the cleaners. You asked me to take it with my things just yesterday," Summer yelled back, tossing magazines in all directions.

Connie screamed.

Summer sighed and pushed herself to her feet, going off to assist her friend.

Connie was nearly hysterical. "What am I going to wear?" she wailed. "Joel will be here in twenty minutes, and I look like Bertha the Bag Lady. Help!"

"Calm down, Connie," Summer ordered, amazed at her roommate's unprecedented behavior. Connie went on dates nearly every night of the week and more times than not did not come home until morning. Now she was having a nervous breakdown over a routine dinner date, for Pete's sake. "Wear your gray paisley silk with the black jacket. It makes you look classy."

"You think so?" Connie asked dubiously, reaching for a dress that she'd spent half a month's salary on, to Summer's dismay at the time.

"Absolutely," Summer declared. "It's perfect. Much better than the red knit would have been."

"My gray shoes! Where are my gray shoes?"

Summer counted to ten and prayed for patience. "One of them somehow fell into San Pablo Bay, remember?"

Connie screamed again.

"God, Connie, would you stop doing that? You can borrow my gray pumps."

"They're half a size too small. My feet will kill me before the evening's over."

"So what? I have it on the best authority that women who limp are incredibly sexy. Drives men crazy."

"Judging from my brother's behavior, you may be right. Give me the pumps."

Summer went back to her room to find the missing notes, glancing anxiously at her watch. Clay was due in fifteen minutes. She stared around the room, then snapped her fingers and dived under the bed. After a few minutes of scrabbling she found the papers. "All right! Way to go, Reed!" she cheered herself aloud, clutching the scribbled notes in both hands, half of her body still under the bed.

"Is there something going on under there that I should know about?" a familiar male voice asked with interest from somewhere in the vicinity of her feet.

"Aaiii!" Summer raised instinctively and saw fireworks and stars when her head made solid contact with the underside of her bed.

"Hey! Are you all right?" Derek asked in concern, hauling her unceremoniously out from under the bed by her ankles.

Rubbing the lump that was forming beneath her silky hair, Summer stared at him as if she could not quite believe he was there. "What the hell are you doing in my bedroom?" she asked him.

Kneeling in front of her, he laughed. "Isn't that the same question you asked the last time you saw me here?"

"Probably. So answer it. Why are you here and— why are you dressed like that?" she demanded, staring at his clothes. Derek had on the most disreputable pair of jeans that she'd ever seen, complete with holes in the knees and white fringe at the bottom above his grubby once-white Adidas. Over the jeans he wore a faded yellow jersey with the letters USC peeling across his chest.

"This?" he asked innocently, glancing downward. "I'm just dressed casually."

"Derek, this is not casual. We're talking major tacky here."

"No tackier than a purple-and-yellow shirt and yellow overalls," he pointed out politely, lifting an eyebrow at her own attire. Once again he'd left off his glasses, and he managed to look so sexy that Summer was tempted to drag him under the bed with her.

"What are you doing here?" she asked again. "I have a rehearsal at Halloran House tonight. Clay's picking me up in five minutes. Would you like to go with us?"

"No, thanks," Derek declined graciously. "I'm not supposed to see you this week. I'm taking the time to think logically and seriously about our relationship without being distracted by your gorgeous body. You've got a cute butt, by the way. It was the first thing I noticed when I came into the room just now."

Summer choked on a gurgle of laughter.

"I just came by," he continued blandly, "to ask if you've been getting the gifts I've sent the past two days."

"Yes, you lunatic, and you're about to get me fired." She frowned at him. "Okay, my curiosity is getting the best of me. What was the empty envelope for?"

"That's the other reason I'm here," he answered, his expression suspiciously serious. "I had to make today's delivery in person. I didn't know how to send it by messenger without being jealous."

Then he leaned over and kissed her so thoroughly that Summer was trembling when he finally released her. "Don't let McEntire put a hand on you tonight, you hear? No friendly kisses. And don't overdo the dancing. You'll hurt your leg again. See you this weekend, Summer. I love you."

With that he left.

Summer sat in the middle of her bedroom floor, her eyes glazed, her jaw slack, until Connie came in with a curious look to announce that Clay had arrived. "What did Derek want?" she asked. "Or is it none of my business?"

"He was just bringing me the contents of that empty envelope I received this morning," Summer answered in a voice that sounded distinctly odd to both of them.

"Yeah? What was it?"

"Well, let me put it this way. Do you happen to notice this smoke coming out of my ears?"

"Oh, wow."

"Yeah. Oh, wow."

THE ACCOUNTING DEPARTMENT buzzed with excitement Thursday morning. Mr. Gleason looked grim. Everyone was expecting a delivery for Summer.

They were not to be disappointed. When an outrageously costumed clown strolled into the office at just after ten o'clock, a huge bouquet of helium balloons in one hand and a gaily wrapped package in the other, the entire department turned and looked at Summer with grins of pure joy.

"Oh, my God," Summer breathed, burying her face in her hands.

"Oh, wow," she heard from the desk behind her.

The clown delivered the balloons and the package without a word and left the office. Summer tied the balloons to the back of her chair, carefully avoiding Mr. Gleason's eyes, and untied the ribbon on the package. No one in the room made any pretense of looking anywhere but at the package as Summer ripped into it. Inside the paper was a small cardboard box, about the size of a small square tissue box. Summer pulled off the tape that sealed it shut.

Squeals and laughter echoed around the room as the box seemed to explode in Summer's hands. It had been filled with the leaping snakes that are normally found in trick peanut cans. Summer wondered for a moment if anyone in the room knew how to administer CPR and was greatly relieved when her heart started beating again on its own. Her fingers were shaking when she lifted out the card in the bottom of the box. Derek's handwriting proclaimed:

Yes, love, I know how to have fun. I only needed you to remind me. I love you.

"*Miss* Reed."

Summer dropped her hand from her still pounding heart. "Yes, Mr. Gleason?"

"For how much longer can we expect to be entertained by this continuous soap opera?"

Summer tried to ignore Connie's muffled giggle. "I have a strong feeling that it will end tomorrow, Mr. Gleason."

"Good. See that it does."

"Yes, sir."

Summer sat back down and dropped her forehead onto her desk, dislodging a paper snake from the top of a pile of invoices.

"Oh, wow."

DEREK HOPED the clown hadn't gotten Summer fired, though he was at the point where he honestly didn't care. She didn't much like the job, anyway. If she lost it, he'd find something else for her. She could work for him, for that matter. He'd like to see her go back to school. She was too good to waste her talent when she could be sharing it with aspiring young performers.

Instinct told him that his determined campaign was serving its intended purpose. Summer had looked so delightfully bemused when he had left her in her bedroom the night before. God knew that leaving her at that moment had been the hardest thing he'd ever had to do. He allowed his mind to dwell for a moment on exactly what he'd have liked to have done with Summer last night, but that train of thought proved entirely too painful.

Instead, he concentrated on the future.

SUMMER SIPPED her coffee very slowly Friday morning, delaying the time when she would have to leave for work. She could not help but wonder what would make its way to her desk that morning.

Connie was so excited that she could hardly contain herself. "I love this, Summer. I really love this," she told her friend. "This is the Derek I knew fifteen years ago, and then some. It's amazing."

"I think I've created a monster."

"Yes, but don't you love it? Really?"

"Fact?"

"Fact."

"I adore it."

Connie sighed deliriously. "Thank God."

"It's driving me crazy, but I do adore it," Summer elaborated.

Connie giggled. "I knew you would keep him too busy to worry about me, but I had no idea he'd get this carried away. I should have introduced you to him six months ago."

Summer thought rather wistfully of the six months that Derek had lived only a few miles away from her and she hadn't even known him. "Yes," she murmured. "Perhaps you should have."

"It's fate," Connie decided abruptly. "Definitely. That you and I met and liked each other so much right away, and then that you met Derek and the two of you tumbled right into love. It must be fate."

Summer smiled indulgently. "And Joel? Did fate have something to do with you meeting him?"

"Of course. It's all part of the same plan. If it hadn't been for you, Derek wouldn't have asked me to serve as his hostess, or even if he had, I wouldn't have accepted. So my meeting Joel at the party is all wrapped up in this. Awesome, isn't it?"

"Totally," Summer agreed gravely, pleased that Connie was so smitten with Joel. Summer liked the quiet, personable man. When she'd first met him, she'd worried a little that Joel was too gentle for Connie, that Connie would tire of him too quickly. But now she thought that perhaps Joel was just what Connie needed to rebuild her self-image and put some stability into her haphazard life without subduing her irrepressible spirit.

Perhaps it *was* fate, she mused as she washed her coffee cup and prepared to leave for work. Already she was anticipating the delivery she knew would arrive that morning.

THE HOURS PASSED with painful slowness. Even Mr. Gleason looked mildly surprised when no oddly garbed messenger had arrived with a delivery by late morning. Summer and Connie were both disappointed. They had been so sure that Derek would send one last message.

"I knew it," Summer muttered at one point. "He *is* trying to drive me crazy." He would have known, of course, that she was expecting something from him. Trust Derek not to do the expected.

At eleven Connie walked up to Summer's desk with a comical frown. "What do you suppose he's up to?" she demanded.

"I have no idea," Summer replied with complete honesty.

Connie sighed. "Oh, well. We'll find out soon enough, I suppose. By the way, Joel's picking me up for lunch and he wants you to join us. Interested?"

"Sure, I'd love to. Unless you want me to politely decline," Summer teased, grateful for the distraction.

"No. I want you to get to know Joel. And he you."

"Then it's a date."

Summer enjoyed lunch very much. Joel was charming. He was thirty-five, never married, serious, but not too much so, and quite handsome with his black hair and mustache and smiling blue eyes. He was also visibly infatuated with Summer's vivacious roommate. He didn't seem at all disturbed by Connie's less-than-circumspect past, but rather seemed to admire her for her unapologetic individuality. He made a very good foil for Connie, and Summer found herself crossing her fingers under the table, hoping that the budding relationship would flower into a serious romance.

Joel was vastly amused by Connie's tale of Derek's unusual courtship of Summer. In fact, something about his amusement puzzled Summer. She had understood that Derek and Joel did not know each other very well, but now she was beginning to think that they knew each other quite well, indeed. She studied Joel more closely throughout the remainder of the meal, wondering if he were quite as mild-mannered and innocuous as he first appeared to be. There was something about him that reminded her faintly of Derek, though she knew better than to mention that fact to Connie.

The thought of Derek distracted her, making her forget her curiosity about Connie's newest friend. Summer couldn't quite believe that the series of deliveries was over. She continued to wonder about the delivery that had not yet been made.

Promptly at three o'clock two packages arrived. Summer grinned when Connie gave a low cheer. Derek hadn't let them down. He'd just wanted to keep them on their toes. Mr. Gleason didn't even bother to scowl. He simply waited for Summer to open the packages with almost the same overt curiosity as the rest of the gaping spectators.

The larger of the two boxes was neatly marked Open First. Summer obediently opened it first. Inside was nestled a somewhat smaller box marked Weekend Survival Kit. She swallowed and tore open the taped lid. She blinked back tears as she silently examined the contents—a small alarm clock with a smashed front and a shredded calendar.

The contents needed no further explanation to Summer or to Connie, though the rest of the observers looked somewhat bewildered. Summer and Connie knew that Derek was offering his weekends to Summer to fill any way she wanted, no schedules, no itineraries.

The smaller box contained a delicate gold chain on which dangled a gold, heart-shaped pendant. Inscribed on the charm were the words I love you.

"Now I *am* going to cry," Connie announced thickly.

"Good. I'll join you," Summer replied. And did. So did half the women in the accounting department.

Mr. Gleason got up and left the room.

## 11

THE TALENT SHOW was going even better than Summer
had anticipated. Crowded into the hallway that opened
off the old ballroom, she had a clear view of the stage.
In lieu of curtains, sheets had been hung between the
stage and the opening to the hallway, which served as
the backstage area. The young performers of Halloran
House waited restlessly in the hallway for their turn on
stage, at which time Summer motioned them to walk
behind the sheets and onto the plywood platform. To
her relief and that of the director and staff of Halloran
House, the troubled youths were exceptionally well
behaved that evening, with only one fight backstage
during the show and a minimum of clowning onstage.

Summer was trying very hard to concentrate on the
show and her responsibilities to it. Her blue eyes focused fiercely on the performers, as if there were nothing at all on her mind but that talent show. Nothing
could have been further from the truth. She hadn't been
thinking clearly since the delivery she'd received that
afternoon. She fingered the gold charm at her breast.
She was a goner, she thought dispassionately. Derek
had won. Hands down. If he asked her to tie herself to
a block of concrete and throw herself off the Golden
Gate Bridge, she'd probably do it. She would live on a
schedule, she would start working harder at her job, she

would do anything she had to do to keep this man in her life.

She loved him.

"Good show, huh?" Clay murmured in Summer's ear as he looked over her shoulder to the stage.

"Very good," she whispered, smiling back at the handsome blond. "You must be proud of your kids tonight."

"You bet," he replied with a dazzling, toothpaste-ad smile. Crazy Clay had dressed in a manner that he considered appropriate for opening night of a youth home talent show. He wore a tuxedo-printed T-shirt, black denim jeans and red, high-topped sneakers with orange laces. Though Clay was thirty-four years old, he looked younger, like a virile, carefree surf bum. Only the faintest of lines around his blue-green eyes gave any indication that there might have been problems in this man's past.

Summer had dressed a little more formally, having chosen to wear a high-collared rose silk blouse and pleated gray flannel slacks. She had wanted the youngsters to know that she considered their production worthy of respect. They were used to the way Clay dressed.

"Have you seen the audience?" Clay asked, his eyes following the movements of the two would-be actors on stage.

"Only a peek. Did Thelma's mother come?"

"Yes, thank God."

"Oh, I'm so glad. Thelma would have been devastated if her mother hadn't shown up tonight. She's been working so hard on that song."

"To be honest, I did some arm-twisting. I told Mrs. Sawyer that if she missed this program tonight, she would be missing any chance of ever reclaiming her relationship with Thelma."

"Good for you." Seeing that the skit was almost over, Summer signaled for Dodie, the fourteen-year-old Cyndi Lauper impersonator, to step behind the sheets and get ready to go onstage. "I hope you're right about this program bringing in some healthy donations," she continued to Clay. "Frank told me things have been getting tight around here."

"I think it will help," Clay replied optimistically. "We managed to draw some wealthy and influential businessmen here tonight. I see Connie brought her brother. Maybe he'd like to make a contribution to a worthwhile charity."

Summer had been enthusiastically applauding the conclusion of the skit, but her hands fell to her sides at Clay's comment. "Derek's here?" she said with a gasp, staring up at Clay. "Connie was supposed to come with Joel."

"It was her brother she walked in with," Clay insisted.

Summer's heart began to hammer painfully in her chest. No wonder Connie had smiled mysteriously while they'd dressed for the show, she thought wildly. Summer hadn't known that Derek would be here, but obviously Connie had been in on the secret.

Now that she knew Derek was here, Summer wondered if she would be able to wait until the end of the show to see him. Derek was here! Only a few feet from where she stood! The long week was over, and the only thing that had changed was that Derek had managed to destroy any lingering resistance she had to him—and without even seeing her, other than that brief, rather weird visit to her bedroom.

"Summer, I asked if you're ready for me to get behind the curtains," a young voice repeated impatiently, and Summer realized that she'd gone into a near trance right there in the crowded hallway. Ignoring Clay's curiously amused regard, she managed to rouse herself enough to resume directing the show.

The *Fame* song and dance was an unquestionable success. At its conclusion the audience gave a good-natured standing ovation. His eyes proud behind his thick glasses, Frank Rivers then took the stage to give a little talk about the operation of Halloran House, concluding with a typical fund-raiser's plea for donations and a general invitation for cookies and punch at a "cast party" that would begin shortly.

In the hallway Summer was generous in her praise of all the performers. "You guys were terrific!" she told them, glowing with pride. She had only been involved in the home since Clay had recruited her eight weeks earlier, but she had grown to love the youths there and desperately wanted to help them find ways to work out their problems. Like Clay, she believed that a sense of self-worth was the best foundation for healthy futures for these kids, and she intended to do what she could to strengthen that foundation. "I'm so proud of all of you."

"We owe a lot of it to you, Summer," Thelma Sawyer said shyly, stepping forward with a brightly wrapped package. "We got you something to show our appreciation."

"How sweet." Surrounded by her young friends, Summer ripped into the gift. Inside the box was an engraved plaque with her name in ornate letters, the date of the performance and the words To the Best Director in the World, With Thanks from the Animals at Halloran House.

She seemed to be making a habit lately of opening gifts and choking back tears, Summer told herself mistily. "I love it. You're the best bunch of animals I ever met. Now go have your cookies and punch with your fans."

"They're crazy about you, Summer," Clay told her when the boisterous young people dashed away. He draped an arm around her shoulders. "Tell me, have you ever considered working with talented young people? With your dramatic talents and your gift of communication, you'd be a natural."

"It has been suggested to her," a deep male voice said from behind them. "McEntire, if you value that arm, you'll remove it from my woman's body."

Clay threw a cocky grin over his shoulder and lifted the arm with haste. "Since this is my favorite arm, I'll take your advice," he told Derek. "I had guessed last week that you and Summer were seeing each other, but I wasn't aware that the relationship was to the dangerous stage."

"Very dangerous," Derek answered evenly, dropping his own arm where Clay's had been. He smiled down at Summer's flushed face. "The show was great, Summer-love. You did a good job directing it."

"Thank you." Her eyes glowed at him, noting how good he looked in his charcoal-gray suit with the pearl-gray shirt and burgundy striped tie. As sexy as he'd been in ragged jeans and tattered T-shirt. "I didn't know you were going to be here tonight," she told him, looking accusingly at Connie, who was grinning beside them.

"I just found out myself this afternoon," Connie answered apologetically. "He forbade me to tell you. Sorry."

"I'm not," Summer admitted with a smile. "It was a very nice surprise. I'm glad you're here, Derek."

"Thank you, Summer." He kissed her gently, and she could feel the tremendous effort he made to keep the kiss under control. Something about the hungry way he looked at her told her it had been a long week for him. Just as it had been for her.

Derek lifted the charm at her breast, his knuckles brushing the softness beneath as if by accident. Swallowing painfully, Summer knew there had been no accident involved.

"I see you got my latest gift."

"Yes. I think my boss would like to meet you. He would probably love for you to be present when he cans me."

"Oh, well. You didn't like that job, anyway."

"This from the man who said I should be more career-oriented?"

"Only if you're in the right career," he countered.

Summer looked at Connie, ignoring Derek's remark. "Where's Joel?"

"He had a late meeting tonight and had to skip the show. He's going to pick me up later to take me dancing," Connie explained. Dressed in a shimmery gold shirtwaist dress of raw silk, Connie glowed from her artfully arranged red curls to her gold spike-heeled sandals, and Summer was well aware that the glow was because Connie would be seeing Joel soon. Summer knew the feeling well enough to recognize it—Connie was already on the verge of falling in love with Joel Tanner. Summer prayed that this relationship would work out for Connie, who deserved happiness as much or more than anyone Summer knew.

"We'll spend a few minutes at your cast party, then take Connie home and go on to my place," Derek informed Summer, then added hastily, "If that's all right with you."

Summer smiled at him. "You're learning," she murmured.

"I'm trying, sweetheart. I'm trying."

Summer could not have said later what went on at the exuberant party in the Halloran House recreation room. She chatted and laughed and made all the correct responses when spoken to, but all she could remember later was the way Derek looked at her with the silvery smile in his eyes. She felt as if she were in some wonderful dream, as if only that could explain the way she and Derek had met and fallen almost instantly in love, as improbable as that might be. She had tried to give him time to be sure, yet here he was, his eyes telling her that she had only been wasting time. The sense of relief was overwhelming.

Derek left her side only once, to procure her a glass of punch. Clay took advantage of the opportunity to tease Summer about her dangerous lover. "How long have you been seeing the guy, anyway?" he asked.

Blushing a little, Summer replied, "Two weeks. Sort of."

"Oh." Clay nodded. "Two weeks, sort of. Very interesting."

She laughed. "It's crazy, I know, but it's also wonderful. In case you haven't noticed, I'm walking on air tonight."

"I noticed," he replied with a smile. "I'm standing here green with envy."

Summer patted his arm. "It will happen for you, Clay. When you find the right woman, you'll know exactly how I feel."

Clay shook his head, looking around the room full of young people and their parents. "It would take some special kind of woman to accept my dedication to troubled kids," he mused aloud. "I'm not even sure I have anything left over to offer. These kids are my life, Summer."

She sighed. "Now I'm the one who's envious. I'd like to know that I was making a real contribution somewhere, like you are."

"I've given you a suggestion," he reminded her. "The kids need someone like you on their side, Summer. Think about it."

"I will," she promised, and then Derek joined them, driving the conversation from her immediate thoughts as he drew her possessively to his side.

SUMMER'S EUPHORIA WAS abruptly shattered during the drive home, when all of her fears returned to threaten her relationship with Derek.

Summer on one arm and Connie on the other, Derek escorted them to his Lincoln. They all slid into the front seat, where Summer snuggled happily against Derek's side and chattered gaily about the show and the generous promises of donations it had generated afterward.

"The parents all looked so proud," she mused, then reluctantly reversed herself. "Well, most of them. I heard one father tell his son that it all seemed like a waste of time to him. That's probably the kind of comment that put the boy in Halloran House in the first place. Clay heard it, too, and I could tell that it made him angry."

"Summer, you can't expect miracles in one evening, from one little talent show," Derek pointed out with gentle logic. "Those families have long-term problems that have led to their children's need for help. The social workers and psychologists will do everything they can to help solve those problems. And the money taken in tonight will finance those therapy sessions for a while longer, so the show did bring about results of one kind."

"You're right, of course. It's just that I've seen the sweetness behind the defiance and bluster in those kids, and I want so much to help them."

"Then you should," Derek told her flatly. "Stop wasting your time in that accounting department and start working with kids."

"Uh-oh," Connie muttered. "Here it comes." She sank down into her seat.

"Derek, I can't just find a job teaching. I'd have to go back to school myself first."

"So? You're only twenty-five. You've got a few good years ahead of you, Summer."

"More helpful advice, Derek?" she grumbled, glaring up at him through her lashes.

"I was merely making a suggestion," he answered irritably.

Forgetting that only a short while earlier she'd thought herself willing to leap from the Golden Gate Bridge at his command, Summer sat up straight on the seat and scooted away from him, almost ending up in Connie's lap. "You're trying to change me!" she accused him heatedly. "Dammit, I knew this would happen. I knew you wouldn't be content to take me just the way I am."

"Would you please answer me one question?" Derek shouted, turning into the parking lot of the apartment building where Summer and Connie lived, his tires squealing as he pressed the gas pedal in frustration. "Why is it that you only smiled when Clay McEntire made the same damned suggestion, but when I said it, you blew your top and accused me of trying to change you?"

"Because you are!" Summer yelled back. "You're trying to tell me what to do, just like you do to Connie."

"Better leave me out of this," her roommate whispered.

"I only want what's best for you," Derek argued. "Both of you, dammit."

"And God gave you the knowledge of what's best for Connie and me, right?" Summer threw at him in disgust. "It must be nice to be so omniscient, Derek."

Almost growling, Derek shoved open his door and leaped from the car. "Upstairs, both of you!" he ordered furiously. "We're going to settle this issue right now, if it takes all night."

"But I've got a date with Joel!" Connie protested, crawling out of the car to stare at her brother aggrievedly.

"He can join us. Hell, we'll ask the whole damned neighborhood to join us," Derek grated between clenched teeth, already walking toward the apartment building as Summer and Connie trotted after him. "Ask them if it's so damned terrible of me to try to help the people I care about."

"It's not that we don't appreciate your intentions, Derek. It's the way you say these things," Summer puffed, clutching Connie's arm as they hurried to keep up with his angry strides. "You always sound as if your way is the only right way—for you and everyone else."

"Face it, Derek, you've been trying to tell me what to do since I was ten years old," Connie said in turn. "Even when I wouldn't see you for months or years at a time, you'd send me letters telling me to live up to my potential, to study and make something of myself. Well, I didn't want your words of wisdom. I wanted my brother!"

"Okay, so I came down too hard on you over the years," Derek answered heatedly, turning in the hallway to glare at the two gasping young women who clung to each other and faced him defiantly. "It's only because I wanted so much for you. Mom and Dad didn't seem to know how to handle you, and I thought I might have more influence with you. I knew you were capable of accomplishing anything if you put your mind on it, but I wasn't sure that I would live long enough to see it happen."

Both Summer and Connie frowned at that. "What's that supposed to mean?" Summer demanded.

Derek blinked as if he couldn't quite believe he'd said that. "As much as I traveled, anything could have happened," he explained inadequately. "Plane crashes, car accidents, whatever."

Connie and Summer shared a puzzled look that indicated that neither of them thought he was telling the whole story.

Derek exhaled loudly. "Let's not stand out here in the hall. Let's go in where we can talk rationally."

Summer nodded her agreement. It was extremely important that they settle this issue finally, she told herself anxiously. Her future with Derek hinged on the discussion that was about to take place. She had to make him understand, once and for all, that, though she was willing to make certain compromises for him, he would not be able to change her into someone else. She was just herself, and if he wasn't happy with her as she was, then they might as well give it up now. It wasn't that she wasn't willing to discuss possible career changes for her future with him, but she would not allow him to dictate those changes to her.

They were less than six feet from the door to their apartment when Derek suddenly stopped, frowning. "That wasn't there earlier," he muttered, his eyes focusing on a fresh scar near the lock on the battered wooden door.

"What wasn't there?" Summer asked him, trying to find what he was looking at so intently.

He pushed her unceremoniously toward the hallway wall, motioning Connie to follow suit. "Stand right there," he ordered them softly. "I want to check your apartment."

"But, Derek, what is it?" Summer asked again, studying his expression. The look he wore now was different from the heated anger he'd shown during their argument moments earlier. He looked hard, cool, rather daunting. She swallowed.

"Hush." He touched her arm in an absentmindedly gentle gesture that made her knees go weak despite her lingering anger with him. "Don't move until I tell you to."

The roommates watched in nervous confusion as Derek moved soundlessly to the door and tested the knob. The door wasn't locked. Easing it silently open, Derek prepared to enter. Just before he stepped inside, all three of them heard a muffled crash from inside the apartment.

Summer jumped and covered her mouth in consternation, her eyes locking with Derek's.

"My God, there's someone in there," Connie whispered, her own green eyes huge. "We should call the police."

"Just a minute," Derek whispered distractedly, looking back toward the doorway.

Summer watched as he flattened himself against the door, obviously preparing to go in. She did not miss the way his right hand slipped inside his jacket, almost as if by instinct. The hand came away empty as a look of impatience crossed his face. Then he eased the door all the way open.

"Derek, no!" Summer whispered frantically, moving impulsively to stop him from going in. He shot her a look that plastered her back against the wall, her heart in her throat. Blindly she reached for Connie's hand as Derek slipped inside the dark apartment.

*Oh, Derek, be careful,* Summer pleaded silently. *Oh, God, don't let anything happen to Derek.*

She had never been so frightened in her life, not even when she'd been hit by the car five years earlier. Only her life had been at stake then. This was Derek in possible danger, and she would willingly give both her legs to keep him safe.

She had known that she loved him. She was only now realizing how deeply that love had planted itself within her. How desperately she needed him. She closed her eyes and tried to calm herself enough to think of some way to help him. She was afraid to leave her position in the hallway long enough to make a call for help, terrified that something would happen to Derek if she moved.

Long moments of silence passed. And then a muffled exclamation, a grunt and a crash sounded from inside the apartment.

Connie squealed in fear and dropped Summer's icy hand. They looked at each other for a fraction of a second, then moved in mutual agreement toward the apartment door.

Summer groped for the light switch. When the light came on, she and Connie both gasped at the sight of Derek dragging a large, raggedly dressed, prostrate body from Connie's bedroom.

He dropped the intruder in the middle of the floor, then looked at Summer and Connie. He staggered as two soft forms flung themselves at him, both holding on to him as if belatedly trying to protect him from harm.

"Derek, did you kill him?" Connie breathed, staring down at the man at their feet even as she maintained her grip around her brother's neck.

"No, of course I didn't kill him," Derek answered impatiently, trying to disentangle himself from the women clinging to him. "He's just unconscious. Connie, call the police."

As if he hadn't spoken, Connie put her fists on her hips and planted herself squarely in front of him. "Derek Anderson, that was the most stupid, asinine, ridiculously macho stunt I have ever seen! Are you crazy, waltzing into an apartment where you know there's a burglar? What were you trying to do, impress your girlfriend like some show-off teenager? Why didn't you just do handstands in the parking lot? Don't you know this sleaze bag could have killed you?"

"Connie, would you please shut up and call the police?"

"No, I will not! I'm not finished with you yet! What if he had . . ."

As Connie continued to berate her brother, Summer stepped carefully over the unconscious body of the would-be burglar, walked to the telephone and dialed the number of the police station, a number she'd carefully memorized but had never needed before now.

When she hung up, she looked around the apartment, finding her portable television, Connie's stereo, a camera and some jewelry piled on the living room floor. "He was really going to rip us off!" she exclaimed indignantly.

"No kidding," Derek responded in exasperation, ignoring the fact that Connie was still raging on at him without even pausing for breath. "Lord, how have the two of you managed to live here for almost a year without this happening before? No security in the building, locks on your door that wouldn't keep out a five-year-old delinquent. This guy probably had the door open in less than a minute. If I hadn't been with you, the two of you would have just walked right in on him."

"Isn't that exactly what you just did?" Connie demanded, his criticism setting her off again. "Of all the dumb, stupid, irresponsible . . ."

Ignoring his sister, Derek threw a dark look at Summer. "The police will be here soon. Go throw some things in a bag. You're spending the night at my place. I'll have new locks installed here tomorrow."

Summer almost bristled at his tone, but remembering how frightened she had been for him, she only nodded and turned toward her bedroom. She really didn't want to stay here tonight, anyway, she told herself logically, stuffing jeans and a shirt into an overnight bag. Even if the apartment were double-locked and guarded by Mr. T, she'd rather sleep in Derek's arms.

In the other room she heard Derek inform Connie that she, too, would be spending the night at Derek's house.

"But, Derek, Joel's going to be here in a few minutes to take me out," she heard Connie argue.

"Tell him to drive you to my place when the evening's over," Derek answered with exaggerated patience. "Unless you spend the night at his house, in which case I want you to call me."

"I am not a teenager!" Connie shouted. "And besides, our relationship is not at that stage."

"Your relationships usually reach that stage as soon as the guy's finger touches your doorbell."

"Of all the—"

"Would you two please stop it?" Summer yelled, throwing her makeup case into the overnight bag. "Haven't we had enough violence for one night? Connie, pack some clothes. I'll take them on to Derek's."

The police arrived, took a statement from Derek with brisk efficiency and hauled their dazed burglar away. "The guy was a total amateur," Derek muttered disgustedly. "Probably a junkie."

"Yeah, and what if he'd been wired and armed?" Connie demanded, his words reminding her that she was still angry at him for risking his safety.

"Very few small-time burglars carry weapons, Connie," Derek explained with strained patience. "If they get caught, the possession of a weapon makes their offense much more serious."

"But you didn't *know* he was unarmed," Connie argued. "He could have been a professional."

"In this place?" Derek gestured around the apartment. "Give me a break."

"Well, thanks a lot."

Summer suddenly laughed, drawing two pairs of eyes to her face in question. "Connie, would you listen to yourself?" she asked in unexpected amusement. "You sound just like Derek when he's giving one of his lectures. If it was him talking to you like that, you'd go into orbit."

Connie bit her lip, her green eyes beginning to sparkle. "You're right," she admitted. "I do sound like Derek." She glanced sheepishly at her brother. "I was only yelling at you because you scared me half to death," she told him. "You make me mad as hell, but you're my brother and I love you. I didn't want you to be hurt."

Derek's face softened as he looked at her. "I love you, too, Connie. Let's start over, shall we? As adults."

Connie stepped into her brother's open arms and hugged him fervently. "Yes, let's," she agreed, her voice suspiciously thick before she cleared it and stepped back.

Derek glanced over at Summer, who was smiling mistily at her best friend and her lover. "Still teaching object lessons, Summer-love?" he murmured quietly.

"I guess it's becoming a habit," she replied, meeting his look with love in her eyes. They still had things to work out between them, but at last she was fully convinced that a solution was possible for them.

The only important thing was that Derek was safe, and he loved her. And she loved him. Anything was possible.

# 12

DEREK INSISTED that he and Summer would stay in the apartment until Joel arrived to pick up Connie. Connie made a token protest, but it wasn't hard to see that she was rather reluctant to stay alone in the apartment with its broken lock. Derek checked the locks on the windows while they waited, grumbling the entire time about the shabby security provided by their apartment. "I'll have to have every lock in the apartment replaced," he muttered.

"Did it ever occur to you that we're quite capable of having our own locks replaced?" Connie asked sarcastically, sitting on the couch with her feet propped on the coffee table in front of her as she watched Derek take his survey.

Her brother gave her a withering look and walked into her bedroom to examine her windows, having already dismissed Summer's.

"Are you sure you want to spend the rest of your life with that man?" Connie demanded of her roommate.

Summer giggled. "Hard to imagine, isn't it? But yes, as a matter of fact, I'm sure."

"Well, all I can say is that I'm glad Joel's not the bossy type. At least *he* won't yell at me for being the innocent victim of an attempted robbery," Connie proclaimed loftily.

Joel arrived shortly afterward, his thick black hair windblown, as if he'd been in a great rush. He apologized profusely to Connie for being late, so courteous and attentive that Summer could see Connie falling even harder for him right on the spot.

"Wait until I tell you about the excitement you missed," Connie told Joel after he had greeted Summer and Derek.

"What excitement?" he asked indulgently, smiling down at her.

Connie rapidly told him about the burglar they had surprised when they'd returned from Halloran House.

"*What?*"

Connie and Summer blinked at the unexpected roar from the man who'd been so quiet and amiable until now. Summer could have sworn she heard Derek chuckle.

"Joel—" Connie began questioningly, but his words cut her off.

"You mean you would have just walked right in on the guy if Derek hadn't been here to stop you?" Joel demanded, his blue eyes flashing dangerously. "Don't you ever check your door when you return from someplace? What would you have done if the door had been standing wide open? Just come on in?"

Connie's mouth dropped open, then snapped shut. "Hey! Derek was the one who just walked right in!"

"Derek is fully capable of taking care of himself," Joel returned immediately, brushing off the implication that Derek had behaved at all unwisely. "But you and Summer are another story. Don't you know that the locks in this place wouldn't—"

"Wouldn't keep out a five-year-old delinquent," Connie quoted her brother, turning a comically resigned face toward Summer. "I've heard this speech already tonight."

"Well, you're going to hear it again," Joel promised her. "This is a big city, Connie. Two women living alone have to be careful. I'm only telling you this because I care about what happens to you."

Summer was giggling when Joel and Connie left. Connie looked so stunned as she meekly accompanied Joel out the door.

"Don't forget to let me know something about tonight," Derek threw after her.

Connie glared back at him over her shoulder.

Ah, well, Summer thought in resignation. As Derek had pointed out earlier, miracles did not happen in one night. Still, she thought the Andersons were well on their way to redefining their relationship, even to becoming friends.

And now she and Derek had to work out their own problems. Maybe now that she was beginning to understand him a little better, the reasons behind his seemingly compulsive advice-giving . . .

Watching Derek wearily massaging the back of his neck with one hand, Summer suddenly frowned as a vivid memory flashed through her mind. Derek flattening himself against the door of the apartment. His hand sliding under his jacket. She'd seen that particular gesture in enough television cop shows to know what it meant.

She thought of the scar on his shoulder. The air of command that came so naturally to him.

"What is it, Summer?" Derek asked, watching her watching him.

"What exactly did you do for the government, Derek?" she questioned him in an odd voice.

He went still. "Why do you ask that now?"

Tilting her head to search his face, she thought of another question she suddenly wanted answered. "Just how did you get that scar on your shoulder?"

He sighed but replied honestly. "I was shot. Three years ago, in Beirut."

She swallowed. "Then you really weren't teasing—"

"When I told you I was a spy? No."

"My God." She was stunned. How could she not have known?

His mouth twisted. "I was really more of a courier than a spy," he explained. "I carried things—messages, money, papers, sometimes weapons—into usually hostile territory. Often there were those who wanted to, er, intercept what I carried or prevent it from reaching its destination. That's how I was shot."

"And that's what you meant by not knowing whether you would be around to see your sister grown up," Summer clarified.

"Yes." He stood very still, allowing her to absorb the new information about him in her own way.

"Connie doesn't know, does she?"

"No."

"Your parents?"

"My father knows. We decided that Mom would worry too much if she knew the truth, though I think she's always suspected. And Connie, well, Connie talks too much sometimes. It was better if she didn't know the whole story."

"And just why didn't you tell me, Derek?" Summer asked heatedly. "Just what excuse do you have for not telling me?"

He looked surprised that she was so angry. "I didn't think it was important."

"Didn't think it was important?" she repeated, her voice rising. "You made me tell you every detail of my life for the past twenty-five years, but you didn't think it was important for me to know that the man I thought was a harmless diplomatic attaché was actually a secret agent?"

"Summer, I would have told you eventually. Soon."

"You had plenty of opportunity. Dammit, we even joked about it. I can understand why you didn't tell me that first night, but why not later, after we'd become . . . involved?"

"All right, I didn't want to tell you," he snapped. "I didn't want you to fall for me because you thought I was a movie hero like the guy you described the night we met. If that's what you were really looking for, then I'm the wrong man because all I intend to be from now on is an ordinary businessman, just as you thought I was all along."

"In other words, you thought that I was empty-headed enough to fall head over heels in love with you just because I would have been impressed with your courage and your daring?" she asked coldly. "That I would think you were a romantic James Bond, who'd sweep me right off my feet?"

He flushed uncomfortably. "No, that's not what I thought. Well, maybe I felt that way at first, but— dammit, Summer, I don't know why I didn't tell you, all right? But now you know. Does it really make any difference to you?"

She looked at him, long and hard, reading the anxiety in his eyes, the weariness in the lines around his mouth. And she loved him so much she ached. She sighed. "No."

His expression softened. "Summer . . ."

She had no intention of making it too easy for him. "I'll get my things and Connie's," she informed him, backing away from his outstretched arms. "I'm tired and I'm ready to get out of here tonight. That broken door makes me nervous."

"You don't have to be nervous while I'm here," Derek told her impatiently.

She shot him a pointed look. "I can't tell you how comforting that is," she murmured, taking great pleasure in the small revenge.

He scowled and shut up.

"WHY DON'T YOU take Connie's things on into the guest room," Derek suggested to Summer as they entered his house. "I'll pour us a drink. I have a feeling we're going to need one."

"Fine," she said, leaving her own things in the den with him. She had no intention of sharing the guest room with Connie that night, though she planned to make Derek crawl a little before she pounced on him. She figured he needed it. One thing about these hero-types, she thought smugly, they tended to be a bit overconfident.

When she returned to the den, Derek was waiting with a glass of chilled white wine in his hand. He had removed his jacket and tie, unbuttoned the top three buttons of his shirt, rolled back his sleeves and taken off his dark-framed glasses, transforming himself from the conservative businessman into the macho ex-spy. Summer wondered how she'd ever believed he'd been anyone else. She forced herself to resist reaching out to stroke one powerfully muscled arm as she took her drink, though she made herself a promise that, before the night was over, she'd test the strength of every muscle in his body.

"About your former line of work, Derek," she began when they were seated on the sofa, Derek rather stiffly, Summer completely at ease.

He sighed. "What about it?"

"Why?"

He shrugged, not pretending to misunderstand. "For the excitement, the adventure. Because I was good at it, and because I wanted to make a difference for my country."

"Why did you quit?"

"Lots of reasons. I got tired. What once looked exciting and daring began to look sordid and ugly. I was ready to trade adventure for normality. As I got older, the daily routine of the regular business world began to look pretty good to me. I've always had a certain, er, talent for giving advice, so I decided to go into the consulting business. The government provided me with the references and credentials I needed to get started."

"And you're doing very well at it."

"I've enjoyed it." He glanced over at her. "When did I give myself away? When I reached for a gun that wasn't there?"

"That was part of it."

Looking contrite, he set his half-finished drink on a table beside him and turned to her. "Summer, I really am sorry that I kept my past from you. I didn't understand that it would hurt you. It's a part of my life that I want to put behind me, a part that I wasn't sure that you would admire or respect. And I'm sorry that I didn't trust you enough to recognize that I'm no movie hero, despite my background. I didn't want you to expect something from me that's just not there."

"Oh, Derek," she breathed fondly, struck again by the vulnerability that occasionally appeared in him to surprise her. "Don't you know you're all the hero I've ever wanted? You've shown me that I never have to worry about being bored with you. That you'll play with me, yet you'll be there for me to lean on in a crisis. I had already discovered all those things about you even before I found out what you once did for a living. My only concern was that you would try too hard to change me into something I'm not, something I couldn't be."

"Summer, I don't want to change you," he rasped, stroking her cheek with one unsteady finger. "Don't you know that I think you're absolutely perfect, exactly as you are? I only want you to be happy."

"I know that now, Derek. And I promise that I'll listen to your advice and then I'll use my own judgment about my decisions, just as you'll do when I make suggestions to you."

"Of course I will."

"Think you can handle being involved with a college student?" she asked him, lifting a hand to touch his cheek.

He caught her hand in his. "You're going back to school?"

"I want to work with those kids, Derek. Full-time," she confessed. "I haven't enjoyed anything that much in five long years."

"You'll be great with them. You'll make a difference, Summer."

"I hope so. I'm a little scared. I'm not sure that I can do it. It's been a long time since I studied for a test."

"Oh, love, I have no doubt that you can do it," Derek crooned lovingly, cradling her face between large, capable hands. "And I'll always be there for you, anytime you might need me."

"I'll always need you," she whispered, looking up at him with eyes like liquid sapphires. "I love you, Derek Anderson. I'll love you for the rest of my life."

"And I love you," he grated, sweeping her into his arms, heedless of the white wine that spilled over both of them. "Let me show you how much."

"Yes, Derek. Show me. Now." She put her arms around his neck and flashed her most brilliant smile for him.

Derek's huge bed beckoned to them when he carried her into his bedroom, but rather than lowering her to it, he set her gently on her feet beside it. Then he kissed her, over and over, until both of them were trembling and gasping for breath.

Summer moaned and burrowed deeper into his arms, her silky hair brushing the underside of his chin. "Oh, God, Derek, I was so frightened for you tonight. Please don't ever frighten me like that again. I wouldn't want to live if anything happened to you."

Overwhelmed by her admission, Derek crushed her to him with a sound deep in his throat that might almost have been called a sob. "I love you, Summer. I love you so desperately," he muttered in a voice raw with need.

"Oh, Derek."

He held her for a moment longer, then stirred against her, anxious to be rid of the garments that separated them. He undressed her with loving care, sliding the rose silk blouse from her shoulders and kissing each inch of flesh that he exposed. Then he reached for the snap of her gray flannel slacks even as he tugged impatiently at his own garments. They were both nude when he finished. Threading his fingers into the hair around her face, he lowered his head to rub his lips over her eyelids and cheeks.

Luxuriating in his tender caresses, Summer sighed. She felt as if she'd known this man all her life, his thoughts, his fears, his pleasures. She pressed against his hardened thighs and smiled at the low groan of arousal her action drew from him. This was her man in her arms, she reminded herself wonderingly, and she had so much love to give him.

He needed her love, she thought happily. Incredibly, he needed her as much as she needed him.

Derek was trembling when he moved his hands to her creamy, upthrust breasts, then lowered his mouth to taste them. Summer closed her eyes and clung to him for support, her fingers curling into his shoulders as she arched into him. She swayed unsteadily as Derek moved slowly downward. Only her hands on his shoulders kept her from falling as he dropped to his knees to nuzzle her inner thighs.

"Ah, Derek," she breathed, finally sinking to the edge of the bed. "You're driving me wild."

"Good," he rasped. "I like you that way."

And then he came to her in a rush of need and desire that drove her back into the soft mattress with a cry of pleasure.

Derek stroked and tasted and nibbled every inch of her eager body until Summer was blazing like a torch for him. Not content this time to lie still beneath his ministrations, she pushed him onto his back and explored his body with the same thorough attention. Derek shuddered beneath her touch, causing her to laugh as smugly as possible in a voice that was little more than a ragged exhale.

Unable to hold back any longer, he twisted until she was beneath him again, making a place for himself between her thighs. Summer welcomed him with a murmur of encouragement.

"I love you, Summer," he whispered, even as he surged into her.

"I love you, Derek," she managed before the power of speech left her entirely.

In the lovemaking that followed, Summer found a degree of physical exhilaration such as she had never experienced before—not even before her accident. She had once thought that dancing provided the ultimate physical freedom, as close to flying as possible without leaving the ground. Then Derek led her into a dramatic climax that gave her the sensation of spinning through space, weightless, carefree, unhampered by old injuries or fears. Freedom.

Much, much later Derek stirred against the pillow, pulling Summer closer to his side as they snuggled together beneath the geometric print bedspread. "Lady, you are good," Derek murmured with gently teasing approval.

Summer smiled against his damp shoulder. "Thank you," she answered primly. "You're not bad yourself, Derek."

"Olympic-class?"

"Not amateur." She lifted her head to kiss his jaw. "Definitely not amateur."

"Well, this old pro is about to sign an exclusive contract. For life."

"That sounds nice," she told him warmly. "Very nice."

"Just don't expect many more weeks like this past one," he warned her. "I'm really a very conservative kind of guy, you understand."

"Mmm." She rubbed her cheek against his shoulder, reserving comment on his questionable statement.

And then she lifted her head with a frown as a sudden thought occurred to her. "Speaking of conservative guys, what happened to Joel tonight?" she demanded.

Derek laughed softly but feigned ignorance. "What do you mean?"

"You know damn well what I mean. Just how long have you known Joel Tanner, Derek?"

"Six or seven years," Derek replied casually.

"How did you meet him?"

"Let's just say we were business associates."

"*Joel* was a spy?" Summer gasped, falling back against the pillows.

"Courier, Summer."

She shook her head, dazed. "I can't believe it. And he seemed like such a gentle, sweet man."

"You wouldn't have called him gentle or sweet if you'd seen the way he saved my neck in Beirut three years ago," Derek informed her, absently rubbing his scarred shoulder. "Joel's got a bit of a temper, you see."

"So that's why you thought it was so funny that Connie was dating him. He's just like you!"

Derek laughed. "We're not that much alike. But Joel won't let Connie walk all over him like that wimpy ex-husband of hers did. She needs a strong man like Joel to keep up with her. He'll treat her very well, but he'll know when—and how—to draw the line when it's necessary."

"You are a devious man, Derek Anderson."

"I didn't plan this, Summer. Joel and I got out of our government jobs at about the same time. He asked me to help him set up his accounting firm, and I did. He really was a client. I never expected him to fall for Connie at my party, but when they hit it off so well, I realized they made a good couple. Who knows, they might even decide to make it permanent, like we did."

"Did we?" Summer murmured with a secret smile, fully aware that there was one question Derek had not yet asked.

"Damn straight," he answered cheerfully. He settled her back against his shoulder and kissed the top of her head.

"How do you feel about children, Summer-love?" Derek inquired blandly after a few minutes of contented silence.

"Children," she repeated thoughtfully. "As in ours?"

"Umm. Eventually. When you finish school."

"Definitely worth consideration," she told him gravely, dropping a kiss on his jaw.

"I might even let them make their own decisions, once in a while," Derek quipped with wry self-humor.

"I'm sure they'll appreciate it," she murmured, already picturing the battles sure to take place in the Anderson home when their daughter became a teenager. Summer was enthralled with her vision of the future.

"When will you marry me?"

She smiled brightly. "I wondered when you would get around to asking me."

"So answer me. When?"

"One month."

"That long?" he asked, dismayed.

"Our families are going to be in shock as it is," she pointed out. "We've only known each other for two weeks."

"I'd have married you last weekend if you hadn't been so damned stubborn about giving me time to think," he growled. "All right, Summer-love, you have one month. Not a day longer, you hear?"

"I hear, darling. One month."

She snuggled against him once more, then lifted her head again with a frown.

"Now what is it?" Derek asked.

"You're sure my leg doesn't bother you?"

"Dammit, Summer. Of course it bothers me. For your sake, not for mine. It tears me up to think of you bleeding and in pain, and of the sacrifices you had to make. I wish for your sake it had never happened, but it doesn't make the least bit of difference in my feelings for you. Would it matter to you if *I* were the one with the game leg?"

"No, of course not. But you love sports so much."

"I've participated in sports over the years because it was a good way to keep in shape for my work and to work off the tension that was an inherent part of my job. It also made a good cover. You can't imagine how many deliveries I made in smoke-filled arenas and sweat-rank gyms. Even at checkpoints in marathon races. But I'm not going to leave you on the sidelines now that I've found you, my love. As a matter of fact," he added, his hand straying to her breast, "I can think of several interesting sports we can take up together."

"Mmm. I like the way you think," she purred, finally allowing herself to be convinced that Derek did not see her as a burden or an object of pity.

"If it makes you feel any better, I'll even tolerate a few gimp jokes. I still don't think they're particularly funny, but I'd hate for you to go back to thinking I'm a stuffed shirt."

"Oh, Derek, I love you." She rolled on top of him to cover his face with kisses. "I'll never call you a stuffed shirt again."

He laughed and hugged her close. "Didn't I warn you once about making promises you might not be able to keep."

A sinuous wriggle was her only reply. Derek's grin faded as desire returned with breathtaking abruptness. He rolled on top of her and crushed her erotically into the pillows.

Summer murmured her pleasure and responded wholeheartedly.

When the telephone rang, Derek cursed softly and flopped onto his back, covering his eyes with his forearm. "My sister has lousy timing," he muttered.

"You're the one who demanded that she call," Summer teased breathlessly, reaching for the telephone. "Hello?"

"Hi, Summer. Did I catch you at an inconvenient moment?" Connie's voice asked hopefully.

"You might say that," Summer replied dryly. "I take it you're not spending the night here tonight?"

"You got it. Think Derek will be mad?"

Summer eyed her impatient lover. "Nope. Does this mean that Joel's not still mad at you for almost being robbed?"

Connie sighed audibly. "Can you believe it? I had no idea I was getting involved with the Incredible Hulk. Remind me to try not to make him angry very often, will you?"

"You could always stop seeing him," Summer suggested impishly.

"No way. I seem to have a weakness for bossy men. And if you tell Derek I said that, I'll swear you lied."

Summer laughed and promised to keep quiet. "Besides," she added, "I seem to have the same weakness."

"Yeah. Who'd a believed it?" Connie paused, then spoke again. "By the way, Summer, I think you and I need to have a talk with these two guys about what they used to do before they became respectable businessmen."

Summer grinned. She'd known Connie wouldn't be fooled for long. Derek had a tendency to underestimate his sister's intelligence. "We'll do that. Good night, Connie. Have fun."

Connie giggled. "You, too, kid. Bye."

Summer replaced the receiver and turned to Derek. "Connie's staying at Joel's tonight."

"That decision," Derek replied unconcernedly, "is entirely up to her."

"My, my," Summer drawled. "Is this Derek the Dictator speaking?"

"Umm. See what you've done to me?"

A tantalizing smile played around the corners of her kiss-swollen mouth as Summer looked at his tousled hair, which once again was displaying an endearing tendency to curl, his gleaming silver eyes and his almost boyish grin. She remembered the grim memories that had been in his eyes when she'd first met him, understanding now what had put them there. He had needed her in his life then, just as she had needed him. "I like what I've done to you," she told him, no longer teasing.

"So do I, Summer-love. So do I."

He pulled her down beside him and began to demonstrate quite thoroughly just how much he loved her.

"JUST LOOK AT the two of them standing there."

In response to Connie's grumble, Summer turned her head and looked across the room to where Derek and Joel stood in quiet conversation in front of the impressive glass wall of Derek's living room. All around them the room was filled with chattering, laughing guests in brightly colored garments. Derek wore a beautifully tailored suit of a light gray fabric almost exactly the color of his eyes; Joel had chosen to wear navy. They looked exactly like two respectable, dignified businessmen. Summer turned back to her former roommate, tilting her head so that she could look up at the taller woman from beneath the small, net-trimmed brim of her white hat. "They look like a couple of stuffed shirts, don't they?" she murmured with a laugh.

Connie sighed, straightening the full skirt of her emerald-green bridesmaid's dress. "That's exactly what we would have thought only a few months ago. What happened to us, Summer?"

"We were conned," Summer answered without hesitation. "Completely taken in by a couple of mild-mannered businessmen with the souls of adventurers."

"They wear their disguises well," Connie mused, turning her gaze back across the room to look lovingly at the two men who'd made such changes in her life and Summer's.

"Very well, indeed," Summer agreed. "Excuse me, Connie, my mother's trying to have a conversation with Clay. I think she might need rescuing."

Connie grinned. "Your scheme to fix Clay up with Autumn certainly bombed, didn't it?"

"Did it ever. They've been chatting like old buddies from the minute they met. No chemistry at all."

"Ah, well. Maybe you can fix him up with Spring when she's able to visit you." To everyone's disappointment Spring had come down with a minor illness that prevented her joining the rest of her family for the wedding, but she had promised to visit Summer and Derek in a few months.

Summer burst into laughter. "Now *that* would be funny." Her eyes danced as she thought of her quiet sister paired with Crazy Clay.

Derek turned in the direction of Summer's laughter, his heart warmed, as always, by the musical sound. He could feel his mouth tilting into a besotted smile at the sight of the petite, glowing woman who had been his wife for almost half an hour. She looked so beautiful in her mother's antique lace, tea-length wedding gown

Already he was counting the minutes until he could be alone with her.

"I don't know about you, but I always start to worry when the two of them laugh like that," Joel murmured at Derek's side. "What do you suppose they're planning?"

"I don't know," Derek replied with his piratical grin. "But, whatever it is, we can handle it, my friend. Excuse me."

His long, confident strides moved him quickly through the crowded room to his wife's side. He smiled at his thoroughly charmed mother-in-law as he slipped his arm around Summer's waist. "You and Connie weren't laughing at Joel and me a few moments ago, were you, Summer-love?" he asked her softly.

She looked at him with innocent blue eyes. "Why, Derek, would we do that?"

He chuckled. "Frequently."

"So," she challenged him lovingly, "what are you going to do about it?"

With a quick glance at her mother Derek leaned over and whispered into his wife's ear exactly what he planned to do about it. His suggestion was definitely at odds with his appearance of utter respectability.

Blushing scarlet, Summer smiled in eager anticipation.

# *Harlequin Temptation*

# COMING NEXT MONTH

### #177 TEST OF TIME Jayne Ann Krentz

New bride Katy was thrilled by her husband's ardor and by the prospect of sharing a lifetime with him. Too soon she discovered the real reason Garrett had married her....

### #178 WIT AND WISDOM Shirley Larson

For a man whose lovemaking was more than eloquent, Joel was tongue-tied when it came to those three little words Alison longed to hear. It was high time to persuade him that words could speak as loudly as actions....

### #179 ONE OF THE FAMILY Kristine Rolofson

Allie had just popped into the post office to pick up a few letters—and ended up with one angry male! But even though her rambunctious kids had accidentally destroyed his bicycle, Michael quickly saw the advantages to being stranded....

### #180 BEFORE AND AFTER Mary Jo Territo

Verna Myers found the willpower to shed some pounds, and chose a spa to do the job. Then robust fellow guest Mel Hopkins made an unintentionally grand entrance into her life. And Verna suspected food would not be her only temptation....

# Harlequin Intrigue
## Adopts a New Cover Story!

We are proud to present to you
the new Harlequin Intrigue cover design.

Look for two exciting new stories each month, which
mix a contemporary, sophisticated romance with the
surprising twists and turns of a puzzler . . . romance
with "something more."

# Take 4 best-selling love stories FREE
## Plus get a FREE surprise gift!